EDDIE ALBERT

AND THE AMAZING ANIMAL GANG

The Curse of the Smugglers' Treasure

BOOKS BY PAUL O'GRADY

Eddie Albert and the Amazing Animal Gang

The Amsterdam Adventure

The Curse of the Smugglers' Treasure

EDDIE ALBERT

AND THE AMAZING ANIMAL GANG

The Curse of the Smugglers' Treasure

PAUL O'GRADY

ILLUSTRATED BY SUE HELLARD

HarperCollins *Children's Books*

First published in the United Kingdom by
HarperCollins *Children's Books* in 2022
Published in this edition in 2023
HarperCollins *Children's Books* is a division of HarperCollins*Publishers* Ltd
1 London Bridge Street
London SE1 9GF

www.harpercollins.co.uk

HarperCollins*Publishers*
Macken House, 39/40 Mayor Street Upper,
Dublin 1, D01 C9W8, Ireland

1

ISBN 978-0-00-844687-1

Paul O'Grady and Sue Hellard assert the moral right to be identified as the
author and illustrator of the work respectively

A CIP catalogue record for this title is available from the British Library.
Typeset in Arno Pro 12pt by Sorrel Packham
Printed and bound in the UK using 100% renewable electricity
at CPI Group (UK) Ltd

This book is produced from independently certified FSC™ paper
to ensure responsible forest management.

For more information visit: www.harpercollins.co.uk/green

For Abel and Halo

EDDIE

THE RANCID TWINS

AUNT BUDGE

FLO

MONSIEUR LOUIS LAPIN

BUNTY

STANLEY

DAN AND JAKE

BUTCH

PROLOGUE

If alarm clocks had feelings, then Eddie Albert's would have been disappointed to find that sounding its alarm had been a waste of time, as Eddie had been up, washed and dressed for ages. This was unusual behaviour for Eddie as normally of a morning he was slow to wake up, preferring to press the snooze button and roll over for another ten minutes under his duvet.

His dad would shout up the stairs telling him that if he didn't get a move on, his Weetabix would go soggy and he'd be late for school.

Eddie would shout back, 'I'm up, Dad!', craftily slide a leg out of bed and stamp on the floor with his foot, thinking that his dad would believe he was out of bed and walking around.

Eddie's dad was wise to the trick, though. He'd once crept quietly upstairs, avoiding the bottom stair, which creaked, and standing in the doorway of Eddie's bedroom, he'd caught him at it.

This morning was different, though, and the reason he was awake earlier than usual was because he'd arranged to meet his new friend on the way to school.

Eddie didn't have that many friends, so making a new friend, especially one so interesting and different, was something very special, and he didn't want to be late.

'You're eager today,' Eddie's dad said, watching him gobble down his breakfast. 'What's the rush?'

'I'm meeting a friend on the way,' Eddie told him as he let himself out of the front door. 'His name's Rusty.'

'Oh,' his dad replied from the kitchen. 'Does he go to your school then?'

'No,' Eddie said. 'But he lives close by,' and he closed the door quickly behind him in case his dad started asking any more questions. His new school wasn't that far away, and he usually took a shortcut through the park, but this morning he'd arranged to meet his friend Rusty on the bench by the tree.

*

Eddie had only just sat down on the bench when Rusty suddenly appeared.

'Oh! You frightened the life out of me, creeping up like that,' Eddie exclaimed, moving up the bench so Rusty could sit down.

'Sorry,' Rusty replied. 'Force of habit, I suppose. Anyway, how's things with you, buddy? All prepared for your holiday?'

'Yes, I can't wait,' Eddie said. 'Only a few more days to go.'

They sat chatting for a while until they saw someone

approaching along the path. Rusty, being extremely shy by nature, leapt up off the bench and hid behind a tree until the man had passed by.

'I know him,' Rusty said, sitting down again next to Eddie. 'He lives in one of those houses across the park and now he's set off for work I can take myself down there and have a look in his bins.'

'Best of luck,' Eddie shouted as Rusty set off across the park. 'See you when I get back!'

'You bet,' Rusty replied. 'And enjoy your holiday. Where was it you said you were going again?'

'The Romney Marshes. They're in Kent.'

'Never heard of them,' Rusty remarked as he shuffled into the bushes.

He really is a magnificent-looking fox, Eddie thought as he watched him vanish out of sight. And quite chatty once you got to know him. But then, being able to talk to animals, Eddie found almost every animal he encountered to be 'quite chatty'.

CHAPTER ONE

Have you ever heard of the Romney Marshes? It's an interesting place with a history of smugglers, pirates and strange goings-on. Maybe you live in the area or perhaps you've even been there on holiday. The Romney Marshes are in Kent and they stretch along the coast from Hythe all the way to the ancient town of Rye. It's not really what you'd call a marsh at all. Instead you'll find lots of flat fields dotted with sheep, winding roads and little villages. Don't worry, this isn't a geography lesson, and anyway Aunt Budge will probably fill you in on all the details as the story goes on.

Do you remember Aunt Budge? Otherwise known as Lady Buddleia Sprockett? Well, she's Eddie's aunt, and during last year's summer holidays he went to stay with her in her house in Amsterdam. Eddie had never met his aunt before this and he'd wrongly assumed that she'd be a miserable old lady who stank of cats and peppermints, and who moaned all day. However,

Aunt Budge was nothing like that. As apart from not having a cat or a fondness for sucking peppermints, hadn't she abseiled through the roof of a laboratory (along with Miss Schmidt, her cook) and rescued Eddie from the evil Dr Lockjaw and the equally rotten-to-the-core, Vera van Loon? But that's another story . . .

Aunt Budge was a quite exceptional lady. Why, she even possessed the same special gift as Eddie – the ability to talk to and understand animals, although Aunt Budge wasn't as fluent as Eddie. For instance, she couldn't understand a word of Frog or Toad.

'Just a load of boring croaks, as far as I'm concerned,' she would say irritably. 'Quite frankly, I'd hardly call them witty conversationalists.'

Nor was she very good when it came to Alpaca or Llama, although she did know a bit of Camel, which had come in very handy when she'd gone on archaeological digs in Egypt with her late husband.

Eddie, however, seemed

to be able to talk to every species under the sun. He could understand everything – from a goldfish to an orangutan – but it was a talent that he preferred to keep very much to himself.

You see, Eddie didn't want to stand out from the crowd, and if his secret came out, then he knew that his life would change dramatically, and he certainly didn't want that. There were only a few people who knew about his gift. He hadn't even told his dad yet, although he knew that he'd have to tell him one day.

Eddie thought about things like that when he was lying in bed. He often wondered what he was going to do when he left school. His Dutch friend, Flo, who lived in the house next to Aunt Budge's in Amsterdam, had suggested that when he was older, Eddie would be able to put his talents to good use. He could work in animal sanctuaries all over the world and then the sick animals would be able to tell him what was wrong with them, and he'd help them to get better. Eddie thought it was a great idea, but until then, he was happy to remain plain old, perfectly ordinary, ten-year-old-going-on-eleven Eddie Albert, who just happened to be good with animals. Nothing unusual in that, he'd say to himself as he drifted off to sleep, lots of people are good with animals . . .

CHAPTER TWO

When Aunt Budge was a little girl she would stay in a holiday cottage on the outskirts of a village on the Romney Marshes. She remembered long hot summers playing in the fields, and the cottage with its thatched roof, and cool kitchen with its flagstone floor, and chickens strolling nonchalantly in and out of the door, having a quick peck or two for any crumbs. She'd cycle to Dymchurch with a large group of kids for ice creams and they'd park their bikes and sit on the beach to eat them. She'd never been happier, and despite owning a grand house in Amsterdam, as well as a smart townhouse in Mayfair, that little cottage was the one she always dreamed about when she was asleep in bed.

One day, many years later, when Aunt Budge was sitting in the hairdresser's having her hair blow-dried, she saw a 'cottage for sale' advert in the magazine she was flicking through. As she read the description of the cottage, she knew that it was the very same one she had stayed in all those years ago.

'Seriously in need of renovation,' she read out loud to herself.

'Oh, I wouldn't say that,' the hairdresser said, thinking she was talking to him. 'I'd say you're in excellent condition for your age.'

Aunt Budge stared into the mirror in front of her and gave the hairdresser standing behind her a look that could cut through concrete.

'I wasn't talking to you,' she said. 'Nor was I referring to myself. I was thinking aloud about this dear old cottage that's for sale in this magazine.'

'Oops, sorry, Lady Buddleia,' the hairdresser replied apologetically, turning bright red. 'I just thought—'

Aunt Budge cut him off mid-sentence and, laughing, she said, 'That's quite all right, my dear. I'm not an old crock yet, but thank you for thinking that I'm in excellent condition. Even if you do make me sound like a second-hand car.'

'So then, this old cottage for sale,' said the hairdresser, quickly changing the subject. 'Are you interested in it? I've often fancied a place in the countryside myself. Be nice to get out of the city for a bit of fresh air.'

Aunt Budge thought for a moment. A memory of a postman pulling up at the gate of the cottage on his bicycle suddenly flashed before her eyes.

'Are you enjoying yourself, then?' she remembered him saying. 'Beautiful part of the country, this. It's known as the Garden of England, and in my opinion this cottage is one of the loveliest in the county.'

Now here was the cottage that she so fondly remembered advertised in a magazine, abandoned and neglected.

Aunt Budge suddenly felt very sad and then, sighing loudly, she reached into her handbag, took out her phone and dialled the number of the estate agent in the magazine.

'Hello, this is Lady Buddleia Sprockett speaking,' she said in her poshest voice. 'I'm enquiring about a cottage for sale.'

Of course, Aunt Budge bought the cottage. She believed it was fate, and driving down to Kent the next morning with her chauffeur, Whetstone, at the wheel, she discovered that the place was now nothing more than a ruin.

Luckily, Aunt Budge loved a challenge. She was determined to restore the old place to its former glory, and within a year, thanks to an army of builders and decorators, that's just what she did. A young family who Aunt Budge knew moved in and lived there for a while, but now that they'd moved back to Scotland the cottage was empty again, and so Aunt Budge closed up her big Amsterdam house and moved in, along with Miss Schmidt, her cook, and Whetstone, who also acted as butler.

Aunt Budge had invited Eddie, his friend Flo and all of Eddie's animals to spend the Easter holidays with her, and they just couldn't wait to meet up again and explore the Romney Marshes – although Eddie hoped there wouldn't be any scary adventures like they'd had in Amsterdam. No, this holiday would be different, he told himself.

If only he'd known what was in store, he'd never have believed it possible . . .

CHAPTER THREE

A lot had changed for Eddie since last summer when he'd stayed in Amsterdam. It had been quite an adventure, saving a baby orangutan from that dreadful woman Vera van Loon, and nearly having the top of his head opened up by a scary doctor. He'd also made a good friend in Flo, whose mother was Brazilian and her father Dutch. Her full name was Floortje Anna Maria Antonia Uffen. 'But everyone calls me Flo,' she'd explained. Flo was feisty, outspoken, loyal and brave, and one of the few people that Eddie could trust with his secret.

Since they'd last met up, they'd kept in touch via FaceTime and Zoom until their dads had both shouted up the stairs to tell them that they'd been 'spending far too much time on that tablet', and that they'd 'better put it away now and get ready for bed'.

Eddie and Flo were attending what Eddie's dad referred to as 'Big School' now, so they had lots to talk about, such as what teachers they liked and didn't like, their favourite lessons and the new friends they'd made. In fact, they'd chat about everything and anything. Both of them had joined the school band. Eddie's dad was a musician and Eddie was following in his footsteps by learning to play the guitar. Meanwhile, Flo was learning to play the trumpet.

Yes, things certainly had changed for Eddie as, thanks to Aunt Budge, he and his dad had moved out of the small flat that they used to live in. She'd bought them a house, with one condition – that the spare room was always left free for her so she could come and stay with them, which they were, of course, delighted to do.

The house badly needed decorating, as nobody had lived in it for years, and so Eddie and his dad sat down to decide on a colour scheme for each of the rooms and made plans for turning the small room at the back into a music studio.

'How about orange walls in the kitchen?' Eddie suggested as he looked at a chart with lots of different paint colours printed on it.

'Don't you think orange might be a bit much?' his dad asked, wincing a little at the thought of facing a bright orange kitchen first thing of a morning.

'Not at all,' Eddie replied. 'It'd be really cool, like being inside a room full of sunshine, all orangey and juicy and really bright and cheerful. Go on, Dad, what do you think?'

Eddie's dad looked at him for a moment and then laughed. 'Okay, orange it is. Although I'll have to wear dark glasses every morning.'

Together, they steamed off the old wallpaper and stripped away the chipped paint. And when they pulled up the ancient carpet they found sheets of old newspaper underneath.

'Listen to this, Dad,' Eddie said excitedly as he read out an article from one of the newspapers. 'In 1982 only seventy per cent of people had a telephone. Does that mean a landline?'

'That's right,' his dad said. 'It wasn't until around 1988 that mobile phones appeared and they weren't like they are now – they were massive great things.'

Eddie enjoyed doing stuff with his dad as sometimes he felt more like a best friend than a dad. He felt that he could talk to him about anything, although he still hadn't admitted that he could understand animals and hold proper conversations with them. He didn't want his dad to think that there was something wrong with him and so, for the time being, he'd kept his special gift to himself.

Eddie felt like a proper workman as he swept up the peeling wallpaper while his dad steamed it off the walls. He was keeping the newspapers for his history class and as they talked, he liked the way their voices echoed over the noise of the radio in the empty room.

'Your mum used to love this song. I can see her dancing

around the kitchen to it now,' Eddie's dad said, suddenly stopping what he was doing to listen to the radio. He seemed miles away as he nodded his head in time with the music.

'Fancy calling a song "Chicken Tikka",' Eddie remarked as he listened to the lyrics and his dad burst out laughing.

'It's not called chicken tikka,' he said. 'It's "Chiquitita" by Abba. Your mum loved them.'

'Oh,' was all Eddie could say. It still sounded like chicken tikka to him.

His dad went back to steaming the wallpaper off, still chuckling to himself as Eddie stood watching him.

'Do you miss her, Dad?' Eddie asked eventually.

His dad put down the steamer and, crouching down next to Eddie, told him that he missed her every second of the day but, as she wouldn't have wanted either of them to be sad, they had to move on and remember all the happy memories.

'I can't really remember much about her,' Eddie admitted. 'Just little things that aren't really that clear.'

'Well, you were very young when she died, so it's not surprising,' his dad said kindly. 'But don't forget all the videos and photos and recordings of her singing that we're lucky to have to remember her by. And I'm really lucky because I've got something extra special to remind me of her.'

'What?' Eddie asked.

'You!' his dad replied, making Eddie blush. 'Now, let's get back to work, cowboy.'

As Eddie picked up the soggy wallpaper his dad couldn't help thinking how much happier Eddie seemed these days, less insecure and better in his new school. He'd made friends and loved his guitar lessons both at home, where they had regular 'jamming' sessions together, as well as playing in the school band.

'Eddie,' his dad asked. 'Have you played a guitar solo in the school band yet?'

'Er, no,' Eddie replied sheepishly, busy stuffing the scrunched-up wallpaper into a bin liner and avoiding his dad's eye.

'Why don't you show them what you're made of? Give them a bit of the old rock-and-roll?'

'They might think I'm showing off. I'd sooner play in the group.'

'What?' his dad exclaimed. 'Having a talent isn't showing off. It's like a book isn't a book until somebody reads it, and a guitar is just a piece of wood and some strings until someone picks it up and plays it. You've got real talent – you're good, Eddie, very good. And when you have a talent, you don't hide it, otherwise it's just a waste. Just wait until I get you on the electric guitar.'

'I wish you were coming with me to Aunt Budge's,' Eddie said. 'Won't you change your mind?'

'I'm afraid not, kiddo,' his dad chuckled. 'I'm a city boy and the countryside isn't for me. And, besides, I've got work to do fixing this place up as well as rehearsals with the orchestra. You're going to have a ball down there, as long as you keep out of trouble. Remember Amsterdam?'

Eddie laughed and promised that he would behave.

'You know something?' his dad said, looking around the bare room. 'This house is going to be something special once we've done it up. What do you think?'

Eddie nodded enthusiastically. 'Yes,' he agreed. 'It is.'

CHAPTER FOUR

The new house was on the edge of a park, and it had once belonged to the Head Park Keeper, who used to lock the park gates every night and keep a strict eye on things. Once upon a time there'd also been an ornate bandstand in the park, where a local brass band would play during the summer months, and everywhere you looked there were beautiful flowerbeds that the team of gardeners had kept in tip-top condition. But all that was long gone, and since park keepers were no longer required, the house had been sold off, and eventually, Aunt Budge had bought it. Aunt Budge, as you've probably gathered, was extremely wealthy, and one of her hobbies was buying property, which she then let people stay in for free – people she could trust, and who perhaps couldn't afford anywhere nice themselves.

Eddie loved this new house with a park on his front doorstep. He could walk his little dog, Butch, as well as play football with his friends from school. It was like having a great big garden. He shared this house not only with his dad, but also with an assortment of animals. There was Bunty the hamster, who'd once belonged to an RAF pilot, and who never tired of talking about her days in the air force; Jake and Dan the goldfish, who would have you believe that they were once bloodthirsty pirates sailing the seven seas; and, of course, Butch the Jackawawa – part Jack Russell, part Chihuahua and part fighting machine. He might only be little, but Butch was certainly big on personality, and when he was annoyed he had a fearsome temper. Then there was Stanley the crow, who'd been hand-reared by Eddie when he was just an abandoned chick. He didn't live with Eddie any more, but, as Butch put it, he might as well have, as he was never away from the windowsill.

'Yippee!' Eddie shouted as he burst into his bedroom. 'We're going on our holiday in the morning, gang. Romney Marshes here we come,' he told the assembled animals excitedly. 'Mr Whetstone is picking us up in the car, and I can't wait to see Aunt Budge again and, of course, Flo,' he added. 'She's flying over on her own from Amsterdam the day after we get there. I've just been speaking to her on FaceTime.'

'You seem to spend a lot of time talking to Flo,' Butch said slyly. 'I think you fancy her.' And with that he proceeded to sashay across the room, shaking his little behind and fluttering his eyelashes. 'Oh, Flo,' he simpered, letting out a whistle (which is amazing for a dog). 'I think I lurve you ...'

Eddie, blushing a deep red, started to stammer in protest.

'What's the matter, kid?' Stanley the crow said mischievously. He was perched on his normal spot on the windowsill. 'Cat got your tongue? I think Butch here might just have hit upon a sensitive subject.'

'Oh yes,' Butch agreed. 'He's really secretly in love with Flo.' And he began to sing. 'Flo, Flo, I love you so,' he howled, making everybody wince as the noise that Butch mistakenly called singing was terrible.

'Honestly,' Bunty said, grunting as she tried to get out of her deckchair. Eddie had bought it for her one Christmas, even though it was actually meant for a small doll. Bunty liked to lie in it after her daily workout on her wheel, and although she looked a little undignified sitting on her back with her little legs in the air, she claimed it was very comfortable.

'Listen to you two,' she said, wagging a paw at Stanley and Butch. 'Can't a boy and a girl just be good friends without the likes of you two sniggering and giggling?'

'Aah, we were only teasing, Bunty,' Stanley tried to explain, even though he was clearly desperate to laugh. 'Just a bit of fun.'

But Butch couldn't hold back his fit of the giggles, just bursting to escape, any longer. He fell on to his back, kicking his legs about and howling with laughter. This set Stanley off, who tried to disguise his burst of the giggles by pretending he had hiccups.

'Really, just look at the pair of you.' Bunty tutted disapprovingly. 'You need to grow up, honking away like a pair of silly geese.'

This only made Butch and Stanley laugh even louder.

'Thank the skies I'm a modern hamster with progressive views,' she added, picking up a couple of sunflower seeds and popping them into her mouth.

'Thank you, Bunty,' Eddie said gratefully. 'And in case you two didn't hear her, Flo and I are just good mates. That's all. Nothing else. Now, pull yourselves together and stop sniggering,' and he started packing his suitcase for the trip without saying another word, unaware that Butch and Stanley were winking at each other behind him.

CHAPTER FIVE

The fish, who'd been hanging over their tank listening to the conversation, suddenly piped up saying that they'd had a change of heart about going to Kent as they had a very important project that they were getting involved in and couldn't spare the time for a holiday, so were staying put at home.

'We can look after ourselves, you know,' Jake announced, folding his fins defiantly in front of his little chest. 'We managed all right when our ship was scuttled and sunk and we ended up in the South China Sea.'

'And don't forget, Jake, those seas were shark-infested,' Dan said proudly. 'Millions of 'em.'

'Yes,' Jake agreed. '*And* they were full of ginormous jellyfish as well.'

'One sting and you're dead,' Dan said gleefully, slapping his fins together. 'But thanks to the skill and cunning lessons that we had at Pirate School, we survived.'

'What's Pirate School, then?' Butch asked them, refusing to believe a word of their story.

'A school for pirates, stupid,' Dan scoffed. 'They teach you how to sword-fight and how not to get seasick and how to walk with a wooden leg without falling overboard, just in case you lose one in battle.'

'Dan lost his eye in a fierce sword fight, didn't you?' Jake said proudly.

'That's right,' his brother agreed. 'And that's why I have to wear an eye patch to this very day.'

'Don't be silly,' Butch replied, yawning loudly. 'That's not an eye patch, it's a birthmark.'

'And you're just a stupid Jack-a-poo-poo,' Jake said angrily. 'What do you know about pirates or eye patches?' And with that he bobbed back down into his tank to fill his mouth so he could squirt a jet of water straight at Butch.

'Can I ask you boys something?' Bunty said, quickly sensing what Jake was up to and worried in case things turned nasty. 'Apart from using skill and cunning, how did you escape from these shark- and jellyfish-infested waters?'

'We hitched a ride from a giant turtle,' Jake replied. 'Wedged ourselves under one of his flippers, we did, and headed for home.'

'So, the turtle swam all the way up the Mersey?' Bunty asked suspiciously, 'and dropped you off here, then? In Birkenhead? How very interesting,' she added, like a detective questioning a suspect. 'Tell me more.'

'We're answering no more questions,' Dan said suddenly with an air of authority. 'You'll have to wait till we publish our memoirs.'

'Oh, you've gone and let the big secret out now about our project,' an angry Jake told his brother. 'You and your big mouth!'

'I didn't know it was supposed to be a big secret,' Dan objected. 'Nobody told me.'

'Well, it was,' Jake replied sulkily, 'and now they all know.'

'And when will your book be out in the shops?' Stanley asked, trying to sound very serious.

'When we've written it,' they both sang out together. 'So that's why we're not coming cos we've got a lot of writing to do.'

'Fish can't write, and even if you could the ink would run in the water,' Eddie told them.

'Who said we're using ink?' Jake replied, with a smug expression on his face. 'We're using a computer – so there.'

Eddie sighed and stopped packing for a moment. The fish were being a real pain in the neck tonight. 'You'll never get a computer in your tank,' he explained patiently. 'And even if you did it would blow up and electrocute you, and besides,' he went on, 'Dad's going to be really busy, so you're coming with us and that's that.'

The fish jumped from the side of the tank and back into the water, swimming furiously to the bottom of the tank to sulk.

'Well, if they stay behind then they'll miss out on all the action to be had on the Romney Marshes,' Stanley said, winking at Eddie with a beady eye and raising his voice so the fish could hear him underwater. 'All those tales of smugglers and pirates fighting the customs men, not to mention the buried treasure. Chests full of gold coins, they say it is. Why, I thought the fish would love it, seeing how they're both pirates themselves,' the crafty crow said.

On hearing this the fish rose to the top of the tank and hung over the edge again.

'You said pirates?' a wide-eyed Jake asked excitedly.

'And smugglers?' Dan joined in, suddenly extremely curious.

'Yep,' Stanley replied. 'The place is full of them.'

'That's it, then,' they both chorused, high-fiving each other with their fins. 'We're coming with you. We'll write our memoirs another time.'

'Good,' Eddie said. 'Now that's sorted out I think we should all get to bed before Dad starts shouting up the stairs.'

'In that case, I'll be off,' Stanley said. 'I'll fly down to Kent once you've all settled in. I'll probably drop in on an old friend who lives in the Tower of London. He's actually a raven, but that doesn't bother me. A bird's a bird as far as I'm concerned. It doesn't matter what sort you are,' he added. 'I keep asking him to come on a little trip with me, but he won't as he reckons that if he ever leaves the Tower then all England will fall.'

'Fall where?' Butch asked. 'Into the river?'

'No,' Stanley explained. 'I think he meant that disaster would befall the country if the ravens ever left the Tower. It's quite a responsibility.'

'Oh, in that case,' Butch replied, nodding wisely, 'he'd better stay at home.'

'Right. Well, kiddies, I'm off,' Stanley announced, flapping his wings. 'Have a safe trip, and I'll see you when I see you,' and with that, he flew out of the window and vanished into the night sky.

CHAPTER SIX

'How long will it take us to get to Kent, Mr Whetstone?' Eddie asked, now that he and the gang were safely in the back of Aunt Budge's beautiful car and on their way.

'About five and a half hours,' the old chauffeur replied. 'That's if the traffic is good and, of course, we'll have to make a few stops on the way so Butch can attend to his business.'

'Attend to his business?' Butch yapped. 'Does he think I work in an office or something? Tell him it's called having a wee.'

'Really, Butch,' Bunty said disapprovingly. 'There's no need to explain it to us, we know what Mr Whetstone means.'

'Humph,' was all Butch could think of as a reply, but Bunty was ignoring him and sitting as she was on Eddie's shoulder, she'd turned back to look out of the window, waving her paw at a couple of women waiting to cross the road at the traffic lights.

'You see that lad in the back of that posh car,' one of the women said to her friend, 'well, there's something sitting on his shoulder.'

'Like what?' her friend asked, squinting at the car as she'd forgotten her glasses.

'I think it's a hamster,' she replied. 'And what's more, I think it's waving at us.'

'Don't talk daft,' her friend said, laughing. 'Oh, now look what's happened,' she moaned. 'The lights have changed so we've got to wait again now. You and your waving hamsters, you'll be saying you've seen the Queen sitting on the back of the Number 42 bus eating crisps next.'

As the car passed the two women, Bunty gave them another big wave, only using both her paws this time. Butch, wondering what was going on, leapt up on to the back of the seat and, being Butch, decided to join in the fun by turning round and pressing his bum against the window.

'Look,' the woman cried in disbelief as the car sped by. 'It *is* a hamster and it *is* waving at us, and now there's a little dog as well who's showing us his . . .' She paused as she realised what

Butch was doing. 'Oh! The rude little thing!' she exclaimed and, nudging her friend in the side, she said, 'Put your specs on and have a look, will you?' But by then it was too late, as the car was out of sight.

'Come on,' was all her friend said. 'I think we'd better get you home as you're obviously overtired,' and they crossed the road with the woman trying to convince her friend that she wasn't tired and that she'd definitely seen a hamster waving at her and a dog giving her a moonie.

After a few hours, Whetstone suggested they stop at a service station. He took Butch off for a walk so the little dog could 'attend to his business' as he'd put it, while Eddie, with Bunty in his top pocket, went inside the services. But before he did that he rang his dad.

'Don't tell me you're there already!' was the first thing his dad said. 'That was quick; did you travel by rocket?' Eddie told him that they weren't in Kent yet and that they were at the services, and after he'd been to the loo he was going in to see if he could buy something to read.

They chatted for a while. Eddie's dad was easy to talk to and Eddie really appreciated all the sacrifices he had made so he could look after him after his mum had died. He'd given up on music and as he had no qualifications apart from being an amazing dad and a brilliant musician, he'd been working in a low-cost supermarket. But after realising that he'd be the worst supermarket manager in the country, and after receiving an offer of a job with an orchestra, he'd returned to music.

'I'll miss you,' Eddie said, as they finished their conversation.

'I'll miss you too, son,' his dad replied. 'But promise me, no more adventures. You stay safe and out of trouble as I don't want to be reading about you on the internet again, d'you hear me?'

'Loud and clear, Dad,' Eddie promised. 'And anyway, what trouble could I get into on the Romney Marshes?'

'Eddie,' his dad replied, 'you could get into trouble in an empty house, so be good. Love you.'

'Love you back, Dad,' Eddie replied.

After Eddie had been to the loo, he wandered into the self-service restaurant to see what was on offer. He wasn't a bit hungry; he was just curious to see what it looked like. There was a salad bar in the middle of the food area that was full of dishes containing lettuce and tomatoes and all the things you'd expect in a salad. He leant closer to the counter to take a better look, but then a man came along and pushed him rudely out of the way. Eddie looked up at him angrily, but the man acted as if Eddie wasn't there and instead carried on piling his plate high with tomatoes.

'Excuse me,' Eddie said to the rude man, who continued to ignore him, and getting no response, he decided to head back to the car.

Just as he got to the exit, he heard a loud yell and turning round he saw the yell had belonged to the rude man. He'd dropped his plate, which had smashed all over the floor, sending sliced tomato and Thousand Island dressing everywhere.

'There's a rat in the lettuce,' he was shouting. 'A great big rat just sitting there.' Everyone turned round to have a look, and a couple of the staff were already coming out from behind the counter to see what the fuss was about.

Eddie immediately felt his top pocket and, just as he'd feared, Bunty wasn't there. Rushing over to the counter he

lifted a leaf of iceberg lettuce and there, munching on some shredded carrot, was Bunty.

'There it is,' the man shouted.

Quickly grabbing Bunty,

Eddie ran as fast as he could towards the exit.

'Come here, you,' the man shouted, starting to run after him, but he skidded on a slice of tomato and fell flat on his back instead.

Jumping into the car, where Whetstone was already waiting for him, Eddie yelled, 'Put your foot down, Mr Whetstone, and let's get out of here.'

Whetstone, used to taking orders from Aunt Budge, automatically revved the engine up and took off at great speed.

'Phew,' Eddie said, sitting back in his seat. 'That was close.'

'Would you care to tell me just what happened in there for you to make such a hasty retreat?' Whetstone asked Eddie.

'It was Bunty's fault,' Eddie explained. 'She jumped out of my top pocket and on to the salad bar and this rude bloke thought she was a rat and then he slipped on a tomato.'

Whetstone wheezed as he chuckled. 'I'm sorry I missed that,' he said, coughing. 'I bet your little hamster caused quite a fuss.'

'I'm terribly sorry,' Bunty apologised. 'I really don't know what came over me. You see, I haven't seen a spread like that since the New Year's Eve party in the officers' mess, and I just couldn't help myself. Before I knew it, I'd jumped into that lovely bed of lettuce.'

'We could've been arrested,' Eddie said.

Whetstone, thinking that he was talking to him, agreed.

'Oh, those were the days,' Bunty went on dreamily, closing her eyes and clutching her paws together. 'Being the RAF's mascot was such a wonderful experience. The happiest days of my life,' she sighed. 'Why I remember the night when—'

Butch rudely cut her off mid-sentence. 'Here we go again,' he yawned. 'Another When I was in the RAF, blah blah blah story.' And curling up on Eddie's knee he went quickly to sleep.

CHAPTER SEVEN

It was late afternoon by the time they found themselves driving along the winding roads of the Romney Marshes, surrounded by hawthorn hedges and ditches full of reeds. They pulled up outside a big wooden gate, which Whetstone opened electronically by pushing a button on a small key fob. Inside, and once they'd driven down a long drive, which was really no more than a dirt track, they arrived at the cottage, and standing on the front step was Aunt Budge with her arms outstretched waiting to greet them.

'Uh-oh,' Butch said as he watched Aunt Budge rushing towards the car. 'It looks like kissy-kissy time for you, Eddie.'

Butch was right, for as soon as Eddie stepped out of the car Aunt Budge grabbed him and was busy smothering him in kisses while Butch danced around their ankles, barking furiously for attention.

'Welcome to the Marshes and to Hodgepodge Cottage,' she

said, picking up Butch and cuddling him too. 'How absolutely, positively, glorious to see you all again. I do hope that you'll enjoy staying here as I'm very fond of this old place.'

'Hodgepodge?' Eddie asked, wiping his cheek where Aunt Budge had planted a big wet kiss 'Why's it called that?'

'The reason it's called Hodgepodge Cottage,' Aunt Budge explained, 'is because that's what it is – a hodgepodge of nooks and crannies and crooked staircases that lead either to tiny little rooms or nowhere at all.'

It was a very pretty cottage, the type you might see on a calendar or the lid of an old-fashioned sweet tin. The roof was thatched, and the pale-yellow straw complemented the soft butter-coloured brickwork of the house perfectly; and set as it was in a garden filled with bright yellow daffodils and tulips, in the fading afternoon sunlight the cottage seemed to glow golden.

'Come inside,' she commanded, grabbing hold of Eddie's arm and leading the way. 'You must be starving after such a long drive. I don't know why it took you so long. I suppose there was a delay on the motorway, there usually is, but never mind, you're here now, and Whetstone will bring the fish in. I'm dying to see them again, such interesting little chaps.'

Aunt Budge wittered on non-stop as they entered the house, jumping from one subject to the next with Eddie unable to get a word in as she chattered away.

The cottage was bigger than it looked from the outside. The wooden front door opened into a hall with a slightly uneven stone-flagged floor, and the living room that led off the hall was surprisingly long with a low ceiling and exposed wooden beams that Aunt Budge explained had come from an ancient shipwreck. It was a nice room with three big squashy sofas that looked very comfortable and sat facing an inglenook fireplace that was so big you could step inside it and sit in one of the little stone alcoves that sat either side of the hearth without getting burnt by the log fire in the middle. There was also a small metal door set into the brick wall. 'That used to be an oven,' Aunt Budge explained. 'They baked bread in that once upon a time.'

'Well, thank heavens I don't have to bake in it now,' a familiar voice boomed out. 'My pastry wouldn't like it, and neither would I.'

It was Miss Schmidt, Aunt Budge's Bavarian cook. She stomped into the room and, laying the tray she was carrying on the table, she turned to Eddie and held out her hand.

'Welcome, Eddie,' she said, shaking his hand vigorously. 'It's good to see you again.'

Butch was yapping his head off, partly because he'd seen the tasty-looking food on the tray and partly because he wanted to say hello to Miss Schmidt.

'Hello, little dog,' she said gruffly, bending over and giving his head a rub. 'Good to see you as well.'

Whetstone had carried the fish in their travelling tank inside and placed it on a small table. They were delighted to see Aunt Budge and were dashing around the tank as speedily as a couple of sharks. Aunt Budge (who spoke excellent Goldfish) removed the lid with the air holes in it and was chatting away to them as they leapt in and out of the water.

'Don't worry, boys,' she was saying. 'Whetstone will soon transfer you to the big tank I've bought you from the pet shop in Hythe. It's got a shipwreck and a large skull set in the gravel at the bottom of the tank – you'll love it.'

'Cor,' Jake said, his eyes like saucers. 'Did you hear that Dan, a genuine shipwreck.'

Miss Schmidt, who had been watching Aunt Budge with the fish, shook her head sadly.

'Now she's talking to fish,' she said grimly, smoothing her

apron down. 'Yesterday it was a seagull and the day before that, a mole. This is why I lock my bedroom door at night, just in case your aunt takes a funny turn and attacks me or if a burglar should break in.'

'I don't have what you call "funny turns",' Aunt Budge pointed out. 'And I don't think anybody would care to see you in your nightie, Miss Schmidt, especially with your false teeth sat grinning in a glass on the bedside table.' Aunt Budge added brightly, 'You'd frighten the horses, never mind me or some unsuspecting burglar.'

This infuriated Miss Schmidt 'My teeth are my own,' she exclaimed, curling her top lip to prove it and revealing a set of enormous pearly white teeth. 'Why, I can eat an entire apple in one bite.'

'I don't doubt it, my dear,' Aunt Budge replied sweetly. 'I'd say with those magnificent teeth you could eat an entire rugby ball in one bite if required to do so.'

Miss Schmidt gave her a terrible look. 'I sometimes wonder if I should think about seeking employment in an ordinary, sensible household,' she fumed. 'One with an employer who appreciates her staff and doesn't accuse them of having false teeth.' And muttering something in Bavarian under her breath, she turned on her heel and swept out of the room back to her kitchen.

'I know I shouldn't tease her, but she's grumpy because she doesn't really care for the countryside,' Aunt Budge explained, turning her attention back to Eddie. 'She much prefers the hustle and bustle of the city. It's the quiet of the nights that makes her nervous.'

'I suppose you don't hear much down here,' Eddie said. 'Apart from foxes and owls.'

'And at a certain time of the year you can hear the marsh frogs. They manage to make a terrible racket, despite their size.'

'Shall I go upstairs and unpack my things?' Eddie asked.

'All in good time, my dear,' Aunt Budge said. 'You can do that after we've had our delicious tea that Miss Schmidt has kindly prepared for us, and then there's someone special I want you to meet.'

'Who?'

'You'll see,' Aunt Budge said mysteriously. 'He's French.' And smiling proudly she added, 'And he's also a famous film star.'

CHAPTER EIGHT

If you took yourself off to Hythe, a pleasant little town on the south coast, and bought a ticket to travel on that remarkable miniature train, the Romney, Hythe & Dymchurch Railway, and went all the way without getting off at any of the stations along the line, you'd find yourself in an extraordinary place called Dungeness.

At first glance, as you climb out of your carriage, you could be forgiven for thinking that it was just a large stretch of deserted shingle. However, it's not deserted, far from it, as quite a lot of people live there. Some of the houses are smart architect-designed properties, ultra-modern and sleek and yet not a bit out of place in such an environment. You'll find people living in what look like shacks, bungalows and even old railway carriages that have been converted into really interesting and very comfortable homes. Imagine living in a railway carriage. I bet it's wonderful.

If you've got the energy, then you could climb up to the top of the Old Lighthouse where you can see for miles and miles around, or you could visit the National Nature Reserve. Dungeness is an interesting place, teeming with wildlife and all sorts of varieties of rare plants. You'll find a shingle beach, dotted with old fishing boats that sit tilted to one side, making you wonder if they still go out to sea or if their days as working vessels are over, and they now lie abandoned. Beyond the shingle is the English Channel and beyond that, France.

The sunsets at Dungeness are like no other as the sky turns from blue to fiery red to deep orange until finally the sun sets out of sight and the night grows dark.

The building that dominates the skyline is the nuclear power station, which, from a great distance, looks a bit like a Norman fort, but close up looks like, well, a power station.

If you were to look very carefully round the back of this power station, which I wouldn't recommend, you might stumble across an old house, hidden in a spot where the sun never shines and screened from public view by an ivy-covered wall.

The locals avoid this old house at all costs as it has a terrible history and is now reputed to be haunted by the ghost of its former resident, Old Molly Maggot, who by all accounts was a nasty old lady who hated children and who was rumoured to be a witch.

When they were building the power station, the company had wanted to demolish the house, but Old Molly Maggot threatened the workmen with a terrifying curse that guaranteed instant death to anyone who dared to set foot on her property. Needless to say, none of the workmen would go near the place, and so they built the power station around it, and the house, dilapidated as it was, remained standing.

Some people said that Molly Maggot was over one hundred and ten years old and after she eventually passed away the only inhabitants of this crumbling old ruin – now called 'Wych Way' – were bats, rats, spiders and pigeons. It lay empty for years until eventually the good people of Dungeness forgot about it, assuming that over time it had collapsed. Only it hadn't collapsed, and a couple of new residents, human ones, and not very nice humans at that, were about to move in.

It was dark and foggy when they arrived. A sea mist lay thick on the ground as a battered old van trundled down the road containing two people, a man and a woman who looked remarkably alike. They were Demonica and Dennis, the Rancid Twins, fresh out of prison and, judging by their mood, not very happy. Demonica, who was holding a torch as she peered at a map, was shouting angrily at her brother, who was hunched over the steering wheel as they crawled along the road in search of their destination.

Finally, after a lot of cursing and arguing and quite by accident, as it wasn't on the map, they came across a dirt track so overgrown in places with brambles and gorse that the van had to push its way through, until they nearly hit an old iron gate set into a wall that was covered in ivy.

'This looks like it could be the place,' Demonica said. 'Make yourself useful, and get out and have a look.'

Dennis grunted, but did as he was told. Getting slowly out of the van with the torch he'd angrily snatched out of his sister's hand, he pulled at the ivy on one of the pillars of the gate to reveal a weatherworn plaque that read, 'Wych Way'. Underneath this plaque was a smaller sign that read, 'Trespassers will be turned into toads'.

'This is the place,' Dennis shouted to his sister, 'and a right dump it is too. It's nothing like the mansion that you were expecting. I'd sooner live in the van.'

'Well, I wouldn't,' she shouted back. 'Anything is better

than sharing this van with you, it's like living with a pig. And I don't fancy sleeping on a park bench or ending up back in one of those lousy prison cells that we've been banged up in for the last five years, so open the gate, will you. I'm cold, hungry and sick to death of being bumped around in this clapped-out van.'

They'd both spent a lot of time in prison over the years. At one time, the pair of them had posed as traffic wardens, slapping parking tickets on cars that weren't illegally parked and then offering to remove them if the drivers paid the fine in cash. They'd made quite a lucrative living out of this scam until the day they tried it on a plain clothes policeman and ended up in jail. After their release, they set up a car-clamping business, charging motorists a fortune to have the clamps removed. All went well until they clamped the Queen's car on a visit to the local hospital, and so back into jail they went.

It was their last criminal venture that had landed them in prison for five years, but then pretending to be Salvation Army officers collecting money for the poor is a pretty rotten thing to do, and so back inside they went, and deservedly so.

Considering they were twins, and they hadn't seen each other for five years, you'd have thought that they might have been at least a little bit pleased to be reunited, but no, they weren't happy at all. On the contrary, they couldn't stand each other.

'You are one of the most repulsive creatures I've ever met,' Demonica shouted to her brother. 'I can hear you farting from here. You sound like a foghorn, only they probably don't stink.'

'Ah, shurrup,' Dennis growled. 'It must've been that sausage

roll from the garage. I've probably got food poisoning,' he groaned, clutching his stomach dramatically. 'I could sue them.'

'You can't sue them for something you didn't pay for. You nicked that sausage roll, so it serves you right,' Demonica said, gloating. 'Now, stop talking rubbish and open the gates.'

'Dear me, we must have forgotten our manners during our

stay in prison,' he teased. 'What's the magic word?' he asked, putting on a simpering, babyish voice. 'Open the gates . . .'

'Now!' Demonica snapped back angrily as she was in no mood for games. 'Why was I cursed with such a dim-witted, stupid, annoying, smelly, disgusting twin brother?' she muttered to herself before losing her temper completely and shouting even louder for him to open the gates in a voice that could be heard all over the Marshes, and quite possibly as far as France.

CHAPTER NINE

It was dark now and from the window of the cottage Eddie could only see one or two lights coming from some of the houses dotted around the Marshes. After they'd had their tea, Eddie and the gang were very keen to meet Aunt Budge's mysterious guest.

'He's in here,' she said, referring to the little room down the hall that she called the parlour. 'I'm sure you'll all love him. He's frightfully sophisticated and ever so interesting. I rescued him, you know – he was just sitting there on the roadside.'

'Had he been attacked or fallen off his bike?' Eddie asked. 'What did you do? Call an ambulance?'

'No, dear,' Aunt Budge replied. 'I simply brought him home and called the vet.'

Eddie scratched his head. 'I don't get it. Why did you call a vet?'

'Because he's a rabbit,' Aunt Budge said, smiling. 'Didn't

I say? Oh, I thought you knew. Did I tell you that he's also a French film star, but he speaks perfect English?'

Eddie reminded her that she had.

'Fancy that,' she said excitedly. 'A famous French film star in my parlour; come and meet him.'

They entered the room and there lying on Aunt Budge's blue velvet sofa was the most beautiful rabbit that Eddie had ever seen. He was a mini French lop-eared rabbit and an extremely handsome one at that, with soft light-grey fur and long silky ears, one of which had the habit of falling across one eye, making him look mysterious and world-weary.

'Let me introduce you to Monsieur Louis Lapin,' Aunt Budge said proudly. 'Louis, this is my nephew Eddie and his friends.'

Yawning, the rabbit looked up from the sofa, and after studying them for a moment he said, '*Bonjour*,' in a tone of voice that quite clearly meant he wasn't very interested.

When he spoke, it was with a lazy French accent, as if everything was all far too much for him.

'Nice to meet you,' Eddie replied, slightly taken aback by this rabbit's attitude. 'This is Bunty,' he went on, introducing everyone. 'And this is Butch, and the fish are called Dan and

Jake.' Eddie had carried the tank into the parlour with him as they were just as curious to meet Louis as everyone else.

Louis didn't even bother to open his eyes; instead he just waved a lazy paw somewhere in their direction. '*Enchanté*, I'm sure,' he drawled. 'But please, no autographs or photos as I'm completely and utterly exhausted. *Je suis fatigué.*'

'We don't want your autograph or a selfie,' Eddie told him. 'We only came in to be polite and say hello.'

'Well, now that you've done that, you may leave,' Louis replied rudely, stretching out on the sofa and yawning again.

'Well, I never. What an arrogant animal,' said Bunty, who wasn't amused by Louis's behaviour.

Nor was Butch, who'd started to growl underneath his breath and was muttering, 'Watch yourself, cottontail, or I might just tie your ears in a knot.'

Aunt Budge, aware that things weren't going to plan, quickly stepped in. 'Now then, Louis,' she said. 'There's no need to be so hoity-toity. It's extremely impolite. Why, I thought you'd enjoy meeting my nephew, Eddie, as he's an Intuitive like me.'

'I'd gathered that,' Louis pointed out. 'We've just exchanged a few words.'

'Oh, yes of course, silly me,' Aunt Budge replied, sounding a little flustered. 'Although, I must say that Eddie has a far wider range than I have. In fact, I wouldn't be in the least surprised if he could understand just about every living creature on the planet,' she added proudly.

If Louis was impressed by this piece of information, then he certainly didn't show it.

'If it's not too much trouble,' Eddie asked politely, as he'd quickly realised just how temperamental this rabbit was, 'because I wouldn't want to tire you out, I'd love to hear what happened to you and how you came to be rescued by Aunt Budge.'

'Yes, do tell them, Louis,' an enthusiastic Aunt Budge implored, sitting down and making herself comfortable.

Sighing, Louis slowly sat up on his haunches, his nose twitching with annoyance and making the tips of his long silvery whiskers quiver. He turned round to check that the magnificent ball of white fluff that he called his tail hadn't been flattened as he'd lain on it and, satisfied that it was still in pristine condition and that he was looking his usual fabulous self, he began his story.

CHAPTER TEN

'I was born in Paris,' he said, settling into a cushion. 'My parents were prize show-rabbits who appeared at many grand exhibitions all over France. They were an exceptionally beautiful couple and, as you can see, I obviously inherited their beauty,' he said matter-of-factly without a trace of modesty. 'My first job in showbusiness was as a magician's assistant, a lowly job, but one has to start somewhere on the way up the ladder of showbiz and on to stardom. It was easy work, but I soon grew bored of being pulled out of a top hat every night, and the magician was becoming increasingly jealous of the huge response I always got from the audience, and so he decided to get rid of me.'

'What did he do?'

'He sold me to a furrier,' Louis replied, pulling his best and most dramatic crestfallen face.

'No!' Bunty exclaimed in disgust 'What a terrible thing to do.'

'What's a furrier?' Butch asked.

'It's somebody who makes coats out of animals furs,' Eddie explained.

'A shameful trade,' Aunt Budge said, wrinkling her nose up in disapproval. 'And yet, it still goes on and ought to be stopped. You'd never catch me wearing fur, nor any of my friends, for if they did then they certainly wouldn't be friends of mine any more. Did I ever tell you about that woman in Berlin?'

'No,' Eddie said. 'What happened?'

'Can I continue with my story or would you rather chat among yourselves?' Louis asked, clearly growing annoyed at this interruption and tossing his ear out of his eye and over his shoulder.

Aunt Budge apologised. 'Please continue, Louis,' she said, taking her handkerchief from the sleeve of her cardigan and dabbing the corner of her mouth with it. 'I can't wait to hear the rest.'

'The furrier thought that I'd make a nice hat,' Louis told them, much to their horror. 'But I wasn't ready to end up sitting on a rich woman's head, so I escaped.'

'Wow,' the fish cried in unison. 'That was brave of you.'

Louis nodded gracefully before continuing. 'I fled through

the back streets of Paris, to the only place I could ever call home.'

'A rabbit hutch?' Butch offered, wagging his tail.

'*Non, mon petit chien*,' Louis replied (which is French for 'No, my little dog'). 'I'm speaking of the theatre!' He announced this in a loud, rich, theatrical voice which made them all sit up in surprise. 'There was a play being performed, a production of some old thing called *Romeo and Juliet* by William Shakespeare, and not being able to resist, I ran on to the stage to bathe in the glow of the spotlight just as Juliet was standing on her balcony calling out for Romeo.'

'Oh dear,' Aunt Budge exclaimed. 'I'm sure Shakespeare didn't write that into the play.'

'Of course, the audience roared when they saw me appear,' Louis continued, smiling to himself as he recalled his moment of glory. 'It was a theatrical triumph, a master stroke, the critics called it. Plus, I'd managed to liven up what I considered to be a very dull scene in the play, no laughs in it at all.'

'I bet Juliet wasn't pleased.' Eddie laughed, having seen *Romeo and Juliet* with his school and although he hadn't understood most of it, he realised that the scene with Juliet calling for her boyfriend, Romeo, wasn't meant to be funny at all.

'No, she wasn't pleased. She threw a huge tantrum backstage and complained to anyone who'd listen that I'd ruined the scene for her – not that she needed any help from me on that score as she was doing a perfectly good job of ruining it all by herself. Dreadful actor.' He snorted dismissively.

Bunty was suddenly beginning to feel very tired and she wished that this arrogant rabbit would hurry up and get to the end of his never-ending tale as the urge to yawn long and loud was growing harder to stifle.

'So, to cut a long story short,' Bunty was relieved to hear Louis say, 'I was spotted by an agent who signed me up, and overnight, I became one of the biggest stars in France.'

Bunty breathed a sigh of relief. 'Most interesting,' she said with a loud yawn, quickly adding, 'Forgive me yawning, Louis, but such a thrilling story has left me quite exhausted.'

'But wait, there's more,' Louis announced, holding up a paw. 'I haven't finished yet.'

Bunty's heart sank.

'I was making a television commercial with the beautiful Claudette Antoinette – now she's a real star, a huge French star, a legend,' he said in a voice filled with awe. 'You've all heard of her, of course?'

They all stared back at him with blank expressions on their faces as they didn't have a clue who Claudette Antoinette was.

Aunt Budge coughed to cover this awkward silence and, after gabbling on about a film that she thought she may have seen somewhere starring Claudette (when it was blatantly obvious to everyone apart from Louis that she'd never seen such a film and that she was

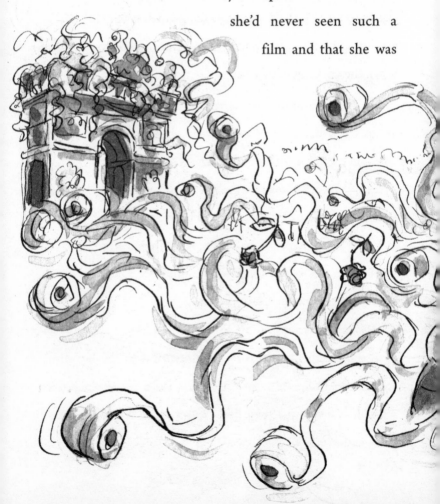

making it up for something to say out of embarrassment), she swiftly pressed Louis to carry on.

Nodding graciously, he continued, flinging his ear over his shoulder again as it had slid back over his eye.

'The commercial we were shooting was for toilet paper known for its supreme softness and which claims to be as "soft as a bunny's tail", which is why I was hired,' he drawled. 'Madam Claudette and I drove down the Champs-Élysées in an open-topped car.

The pavements were mobbed as we drove past; the crowds were throwing flowers at us and we were throwing toilet rolls back at them. It was a truly magical moment. After we'd wrapped – that means finished for the day,' he explained, 'somebody grabbed me by my ears, bundled me into a pillowcase and threw me into the back of a lorry bound for England.'

The fish were gripped by this story and were hanging over their tank, eager to hear more, particularly as it was beginning to sound dangerous.

'Cor,' a wide-eyed Jake exclaimed. 'A deadly assassin?'

'Or maybe they was going to hold you to ransom,' Dan added, equally enthusiastic.

'Well, as soon as we got to Dover, I managed to escape. I'm very good at escaping,' Louis bragged. 'And then I ran as fast as my paws would carry me through the pouring rain. Lorries and cars went roaring past me. How I survived, I'll never know,' he said piously, lowering his head as if deep in thought.

They all sat in an uncomfortable silence, unsure if he'd finished, until suddenly he raised his head and spoke in a grave voice.

'I ran, and I ran . . .'

'Yes, you've told us that a million times,' Bunty muttered under her breath.

'. . . Until I could run no more. Exhausted, I slumped to the ground.' Here he pressed his paw against his forehead dramatically. 'And lay there, limp, exhausted and near death. It was then that your wonderful aunt came to my rescue.'

Aunt Budge smiled and mumbled something about her being only too happy to have been able to help.

They sat quietly for a moment as once again they didn't know if he'd finally reached the end of his story or not and so Bunty, deciding to take the matter into her own paws, started applauding.

'Unbelievable,' she cheered, with a bit too much enthusiasm, clapping her paws together furiously. 'What a performance!'

Louis looked at Bunty suspiciously. Was she being sarcastic? If so, then he chose to ignore her and instead inclined his head, acknowledging the compliment.

Quickly taking their cue from Bunty, everyone else started to clap too. Even the fish applauded, slapping their fins together.

'Bravo,' Aunt Budge shouted as Louis bowed low, wiping an imaginary tear away from his eye and murmuring, '*Merci, merci.*'

'Phew, that's quite a story,' Eddie said, full of admiration for this rabbit. He might have a high opinion of himself, but he was certainly a survivor.

'Indeed,' Aunt Budge agreed. 'It would make a wonderful film. Now, we've got a busy day ahead of us tomorrow,' she said, getting out of her chair. 'So let's get you sorted out in your room, Eddie, and I'll look in on Flo's room to make sure it's all shipshape and lovely for when she flies in tomorrow morning.'

'This Flo,' Louis asked, 'is she a bird?'

'No, dear,' Aunt Budge replied. 'She's a young girl. Now, have a little rest and I'll pop in before bedtime.'

CHAPTER ELEVEN

t took some time for the Rancid Twins to open the rusty old lock on the gate and even longer to push the gate open, which was quite tall and its hinges had rusted up with age. The brambles and nettles that were growing all around it didn't help either, making it even more difficult to move. Once Dennis had finally managed to force the gate open, Demonica got out of the van to join him. The front door of the house proved to be equally tough, and as Dennis fiddled with the key it started to rain.

'Open the door, will you,' Demonica hissed, clutching her coat round her in an attempt to dodge the rain. 'And hurry up. I'm getting soaked here.'

'Give it up. A drop of rain will do you good. It's about time you had a shower,' Dennis snarled angrily and by the time the pair managed to get the front door open and get inside the house, they were both in an even fouler mood than they had been in the van.

If the people of Dungeness had known who their new neighbours were, then they would've undoubtedly put their homes up for sale that very night and moved out immediately, for this horrible pair were the only remaining descendants of Old Molly Maggot.

These two horrors, fresh out of prison, and finding themselves broke and homeless, couldn't believe their luck when a solicitor got in touch to tell them that they'd inherited a house on the Kent coast from a relative that they didn't even know about.

'You are her only remaining descendants,' the solicitor had told them as he'd handed over the keys to the house before getting away from this creepy pair as fast as he could.

Demonica was over the moon as she fantasised about what the house might be like. She was convinced that it was a beautiful white mansion, perched on the cliffs overlooking the Channel, that had endless rooms with chandeliers and lots of staff to wait on her day and night as she lay in bed watching her flat-screen TV. She decided she'd shove her brother in the attic or in one of the outhouses to keep him out of sight. Or maybe one day, he'd just happen to lean too far over the cliff edge and just happen to fall off. She smiled happily to herself as she imagined what she'd tell the police. 'Oh, officer, my poor, dear, dead brother . . .' (sob, sob, sob, blow the nose). 'Such a dreadful accident; he was a birdwatcher, you see, and I did warn him about going too near the cliff edge to look at seagulls, but he wouldn't listen to me. Oh, what will I do without my beloved brother?' Then she'd faint into the policeman's arms for maximum effect. *Brilliant*, she told herself.

She smiled as she wallowed in this dream, convinced that things were finally going her way.

Meanwhile, Dennis, her equally rotten brother, was hatching a master plan of his own. He was going to sell the house without telling his sister and run off to Rio with all the money. There he'd spend his time lying on the beach in a pair of very expensive designer shorts, drinking cocktails and eating lots and lots of burgers far, far away from his miserable sister.

But here they were, their dreams of fancy houses and a life in the sun shattered as they stood in the rubble of Old Molly Maggot's former home.

They were very much alike, although they'd never admit it, as each one thought they were far better-looking, and of a far superior intelligence, than the other. They were exactly the same height, which wasn't very tall, and they both had the same jet-black hair. Demonica wore hers in a short bob with a very severe fringe that made her look permanently angry, while Dennis parted his greasy hair down the middle, letting it hang like rats' tails around his shoulders. Although they were adults, they still dressed alike – Dennis wore a grubby black suit with an even grubbier shirt and tie, while Demonica wore more or less the same outfit, except she preferred a skirt to trousers, which she wore with long black socks that wrinkled round her knobbly knees. They acted like badly behaved children, bickering and arguing over the slightest thing and calling each other stupid names. In fact, as I said, they really didn't like each other one little bit, and yet fate always seemed to throw them together.

'Look at this dump,' Demonica moaned, shining the torch around the room. 'Judging by those cobwebs you'd need an axe to cut through them. It looks like nobody has been in this place since the old girl died.'

There was a hole in the ceiling where the plaster had fallen, branches from a tree had smashed their way through one of the windows and the floor was littered with rubble and bird droppings. They wandered into the kitchen, which was also a wreck with a rusty kitchen range that had a big iron cauldron on top. The kitchen table was littered with dusty bottles and jars and old dried-out herbs. Some of the bottles had labels on them, but the years had faded the writing so it was impossible to tell what was inside. Whatever was in them, the contents of the bottles looked very sinister indeed.

'No point trying to make a fire,' Dennis said, looking inside the range, which was full of old birds' nests, soot and general junk.

'You could always clean it out,' Demonica remarked as she looked around the kitchen in the vain hope there might be something to eat. 'There's enough sticks and stuff to make a fire.'

'You clean it out and make a fire,' Dennis retorted. 'Why should I have to do it?'

'Because you're good with fires,' Demonica replied, maddeningly calm. 'Who was it who burned down the school?'

'That wasn't me,' Dennis protested. 'I was framed.'

'Whatever,' Demonica drawled. 'Just stop moaning. You could light a fire easily in that stove if you wanted to. Just pretend it's the school gym.'

'Ha, ha, very funny. I don't think,' Dennis replied sarcastically. 'And how am I supposed to light a fire?' he demanded. 'I ain't got no matches.'

'You could rub two sticks together,' Demonica answered him haughtily.

'What, you mean like your legs?' Dennis roared with laughter at this; however, Demonica didn't see the funny side, and grabbing an old iron frying pan from on top of the range, she flung it across the room at her brother, who ducked just in time.

'Missed,' he shouted triumphantly. 'Nah, nah, nah nah nah,' he goaded her, jumping up and down and sticking his tongue out. 'You missed, you missed, you missed.'

Demonica was livid. 'You great big stinking cowpat,' she hissed. 'I'd wring your neck if you had one. Why don't you make yourself useful for once and go out and see if you can't find something to eat? I'm that hungry I could eat a dead rat.'

'I suppose I could always catch a rabbit,' Dennis said, rubbing his chin in thought.

'I was good at hunting rabbits when I was a lad.'

'You? Catch a rabbit?' Demonica exclaimed. 'You couldn't catch a cold if you tried, and what are you going to do with this imaginary rabbit after you've caught it?'

'Skin it and cook it, clever clogs.'

'On what?'

'A fire, stupid.'

'But we haven't got a fire, pig's breath.'

'Then I'll make one, fishcake face.'

'How are you going to light it? You've got no matches.'

On and on they went, bickering and sniping at each other into the wee small hours.

A passing rat on his way to visit a friend, puzzled by these two weird guests, made a series of squeaks that, had Eddie been there, he would've interpreted as, 'Oh well, there goes the neighbourhood.'

CHAPTER TWELVE

The next morning, when Eddie opened his bedroom curtains, he was disappointed to see that the Marshes were covered by a thick blanket of fog.

'It happens,' Aunt Budge said as they ate their breakfast in the dining room. 'We can get four seasons' weather in one day here. I just hope that Flo's flight won't be delayed.'

Louis Lapin was taking his morning stroll around the garden with Miss Schmidt acting as his bodyguard. He'd insisted that Miss Schmidt accompanied him as he was worried that somebody might try to kidnap him again, even though Aunt Budge had assured him that he'd be quite safe in her garden.

'I wouldn't dare to put my paw outside this house without security,' he insisted. 'Those kidnappers might still be looking for me, and don't forget, I am a huge star after all, and I can't just wander about like ordinary, common rabbits. I tell you,' he moaned, looking directly at Bunty, 'fame and beauty, and the pressure that comes with being a star, can be a dreadful burden. You should count your blessings, little hamster, that none of these will ever affect you.'

Bunty was fit to explode. 'What a cheek!' she spluttered. 'There's a lot more to life than good looks and fame, although I have had a brush with fame myself after I was voted "Most Popular Hamster in the Officers' Mess", and I can tell you now that the pressure that came with such a position was enormous,' she said proudly, puffing out her cheeks.

Butch was only too happy to go for a run around the garden. 'If any kidnappers show up then I'll ride them out of town, *amigo*,' he said in his Mexican bandit voice that he'd picked up from watching old cowboy films on the telly.

'I'll take you out, Louis,' Eddie had offered. 'You'll be okay with me.'

'You're just a puny boy, and the big lady is strong,' Louis had said defiantly, refusing to move.

Eddie gave one of his arms a quick glance. Okay, he wasn't built like a champion bodybuilder, but his arms looked fine to him.

Louis really was incredibly rude. 'Suit yourself,' he'd said.

In the end Miss Schmidt was called in from the kitchen and Aunt Budge braced herself for her reaction.

'Is there something wrong with your breakfast?' Miss Schmidt asked grimly, giving Aunt Budge a steely look. She wasn't happy at being called into the dining room as she was in the middle of washing up and had had to change her dirty apron for a clean one.

'Good heavens, no,' Aunt Budge gushed. 'Even the Swiss couldn't produce a Bircher muesli as superb as yours.'

Miss Schmidt allowed a faint smile to flicker across her lips.

'No, my dear, all I wanted was to ask a teeny-weeny favour of you,' Aunt Budge pressed on cautiously. 'Would you take Louis out for a little walk?'

Miss Schmidt didn't say a word. She simply stood staring at Aunt Budge and making her feel very uncomfortable in the process.

'Yes, I wonder if you'd escort Louis round the garden,' Aunt Budge continued bravely, shifting round nervously in her chair and suddenly developing a fascination with the spoon she was holding as she was unable to look Miss Schmidt in the eye.

'You mean the rabbit?' Miss Schmidt asked, dangerously calm. She'd been asked to do some weird things by Aunt Budge in the past, but babysitting a rabbit? Wasn't Miss Schmidt the woman who'd swum the Channel – twice? And come back each time with a baguette and a hunk of her favourite cheese in a sealed polythene bag strapped to her back? Wasn't she the woman who'd fought an alligator when she'd worked as a

stuntwoman in films? And now she was to become a rabbit's babysitter, which, as far as she was concerned, managed to top the time Aunt Budge asked her if she'd mind sharing a hut with a group of young baboons in Namibia. *What next?* she asked herself.

'Yes, that's right,' Aunt Budge said, picking at the tablecloth as she desperately tried to sound as though asking your cook to take a rabbit for a walk was the most natural thing in the world. 'You see, he's scared that there may be another kidnap attempt if he went out in the garden on his own,' she gabbled, as she always did when she was nervous, 'and he said he'd be most grateful if you would keep an eye on him.'

'And I suppose the rabbit told you all this, did he?' Miss Schmidt asked, raising one eyebrow.

'Well, not exactly.' Aunt Budge laughed nervously. 'It's just that he . . .' She struggled to find the right words to explain. Thankfully Eddie jumped in. He was used to coming up with explanations, having had to think of believable excuses when he'd been caught talking to an animal himself.

'Of course not,' he said, laughing. 'Rabbits can't talk. It's just he's still very timid, Miss Schmidt,' Eddie explained. 'And he needs someone that he can trust, and besides,' he added craftily, 'he seems to like you.'

'He does?' a surprised Miss Schmidt exclaimed, looking down at Louis who was sitting at her feet and staring back up at her giving her his cutest, 'Love me, love me I'm the most adorable rabbit on the planet' look.

Bunty shot him a look of disgust. 'Oh, pleeeeease,' she muttered, folding her arms. 'Has he no shame?'

'Yes, he's always trying to get into the kitchen to see you,' Aunt Budge shot in quickly, trying to convince Miss Schmidt that Louis was her biggest fan. 'He hops over to the parlour door and cries to be let out – you should hear him.'

'I will not have rabbits in my kitchen,' Miss Schmidt boomed. 'It's not a petting farm.'

Aunt Budge nodded her head in agreement. 'Of course, that's why we wouldn't dream of letting him out. I know how high your standards are in the kitchen.'

'My kitchen,' Miss Schmidt corrected her. 'You may be mistress of the house, m'lady, but I am mistress of the kitchen.'

Aunt Budge cleared her throat. 'Quite,' was all she said, dabbing her lips with her napkin.

'Can I just say that I'm not very amused at being accused of such undignified behaviour,' a highly offended Louis objected. 'I've never cried at a door to be let out in my life.'

'Listen,' Eddie lied. 'He's making little bleating noises – that means he likes you.'

Miss Schmidt still wasn't completely convinced, but to make life easy, she agreed to take Louis out.

As she marched out of the room with Louis hopping beside her, she turned at the door. 'I just hope this isn't a practical joke,' she warned. 'As you wouldn't like worms in your pasta and rabbit poo in your scones, would you, now?' And with that, she headed for the garden.

'I think I'll go with them,' Butch yapped eagerly, his tail wagging. 'I can act as a backup in case anything happens to Miss Schmidt.'

'Just don't go chasing any rabbits' tails,' Eddie shouted after him, but it was too late. Butch had shot out of the door like a rocket.

CHAPTER THIRTEEN

Meanwhile, in foggy Dungeness, Demonica Rancid had woken up in a mood as foul as the weather. She had eventually fallen asleep in an old armchair, and as she'd moved around so much in the night in an attempt to get comfortable, she'd woken up upside down with her legs flung over the back of the chair.

'Where am I?' she groaned, bleary-eyed and aching all over. Lifting her head a little, she realised that she was staring at a ceiling. She was confused for a moment until she remembered the previous evening's events. Muttering to herself, she struggled out of the chair until she was up on her feet again. It had been dark when they'd arrived last night, and she hadn't been able to get a good look at the house, but now it was daylight she could, and she was not impressed.

'Prison would be better than this,' she groaned as she

looked around at the broken furniture and the years and years of dust, dirt and decay.

'Dennis,' she shouted, suddenly remembering that she had a brother. 'Dennis, you great lump, where are you? DENNNIIIISSSS!!'

'What? What?' the crumpled heap on the floor that was Dennis spluttered as his sister's foghorn voice roused him from a deep sleep. 'Is it a police raid?' He panicked, still half asleep. 'Well, they ain't got nothing on us.'

'It's me, you fool,' Demonica sneered. 'Get up off the floor and take a good look at what we've inherited.'

Dennis slowly sat up and yawned loudly. He rubbed his eyes and said to his sister, 'Have you ever heard of waking someone up with a nice cup of tea and a cheery "good morning"? That mouth of yours could drown out sixty screaming seagulls, so keep it shut, will ya?'

Ignoring him, and picking her way through the rubble, Demonica inspected the kitchen. Turning on the solitary tap that hung over a big stone sink, it shuddered violently for a moment before producing a stream of muddy water. 'Great,' she muttered to herself, moving on to take a look inside the various cupboards. She found nothing, apart from a few bottles with something mouldy inside, and in one long cupboard, a number of broomsticks.

'I wonder why she had so many brooms?' Demonica wondered. 'Judging by the state of this dump she didn't go in for cleaning much.'

Absently she wrote her initials in the dust on the top of the big kitchen range as she stood staring at it. She didn't have a clue how it worked, except that you probably had to light a fire inside it before you could cook anything on it. Not that she was interested in cooking – eating, yes, but actually having to cook it first, no.

Thinking about food reminded her just how hungry she was. 'How much have you got on you?' she asked her brother as he came into the kitchen. 'We need to find a shop and buy food.'

'Buy?' Dennis sounded surprised. 'You want to *buy* some food? Don't you mean steal?'

'No, I don't,' Demonica hissed. 'We've only just got here, and we don't want to draw any attention to ourselves.'

This made Dennis laugh like a drain. 'Have you seen the state of yourself?' he howled. 'Talk about not wanting to stand out. The only place where you'd fit in is on a ghost train.'

'You can talk,' she snapped back. 'You don't look so hot yourself. At least I don't look like I've been dead for a hundred years.'

'No, you look like you've been dead for five hundred years,' he shouted back triumphantly. 'So there.'

Demonica closed her eyes, and taking a deep breath and with an extreme amount of effort, she resisted the temptation to lunge at her brother and sock him one. Instead, she composed herself and said, 'There's no point us arguing as, in case you haven't noticed, we're in a bit of a predicament,' she told her brother calmly. 'We're living in a dump, and we've hardly got any money, apart from what's left of the wages we earned in the nick, so if we're going to survive, we have to work out a master plan.'

'Agreed,' her brother replied.

'That's sorted then. Now, let's go shopping.'

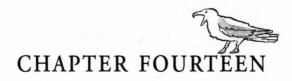

CHAPTER FOURTEEN

By the time Flo arrived at Aunt Budge's house, the sun had decided to show its face and had burnt the fog away.

'Welcome to Hodgepodge Cottage,' Aunt Budge said, greeting Flo warmly by kissing her on the cheek in the Dutch fashion – right cheek first, then left, then right again. 'I see you've brought the sunshine with you.'

'Oh, it's so beautiful,' Flo said, wide-eyed, as she looked around at the garden and at the hundreds of daffodils and tulips dancing in the light breeze. 'And the cottage,' she said in wonderment, 'is so pretty. Like a fairy-tale cottage.'

Butch came charging out of the front door in front of Eddie to greet her, yapping his head off, as he was very fond of Flo. He'd fully intended to jump into her arms, but forgetting that he was just a small dog, he only managed to get as far as her knees. Flo picked him up and, smothering him in kisses, she spoke to him in Dutch.

'I can't understand a word,' Butch said happily as he wriggled about in her arms with his tail wagging furiously. 'But who cares? I'm loving the kisses.'

Eddie hadn't seen Flo since last year in Amsterdam where they'd first met. He'd spoken to her a lot on FaceTime, but now that she was here in person, they both felt a little shy around each other. Eddie thought Flo seemed a bit more grown-up – she certainly sounded it when he asked her how her flight had been.

'It was cool,' she replied casually, even though she'd never even been on a plane before, never mind on her own. 'A lady

who works for the airport took me to the plane and waited until I got on it and found my seat,' she said, trying to contain the excitement in her voice as if she wanted to sound like a sophisticated traveller used to jetting off all over the world. 'I had a row to myself,' she continued, 'and one of the cabin crew looked after me. Not that I needed looking after,' she added quickly. 'I was fine.'

'Was it good fun then?' Eddie asked, eager to know more. 'Was take-off and landing scary?'

'No, it was wonderful, Eddie,' she exclaimed, suddenly abandoning her 'too cool for school' attitude, and instead allowing herself to show just how exciting she'd found the entire experience.

'Take-off and landing were unbelievable, and looking out of the window at the clouds and the tiny houses and canals below was A-maz-ing! Oh, I wished you'd been there,' she said, jumping up and down.

Eddie wished he had been there too, as he'd never been on a plane either and was beginning to feel just a little bit jealous of Flo.

'Then, Mr Whetstone picked me up at City Airport, which is a really cute airport, and now here I am,' she said, grinning from ear to ear. 'Ready to start my holiday with you, Aunt Budge and all the animals.'

And as quickly as they'd appeared, the pangs of jealousy evaporated and at that moment Eddie felt that everything in his world was just as it should be.

Aunt Budge insisted that since the weather had changed for the better, they should eat their lunch in the garden at the back of the cottage, which sloped down to a stream with a meadow beyond it, and beyond that, a wood with a floor that had become a carpet of bluebells.

'So, tell me, Flo,' Aunt Budge asked, helping herself to another cucumber sandwich. She knew they were really teatime food, but she loved them so much that she always asked Miss Schmidt to make some, regardless of whether it was breakfast or supper. 'What do you think of the Marshes?'

Flo took a good look around her and announced, 'It's a bit like the Netherlands,' she replied. 'Flat and lots of tulips.'

'Yes, I can see that,' Aunt Budge agreed. 'But I think you'll find it's actually very different.'

Once they'd finished eating, Eddie asked Flo to come and meet Louis who was lying on the sofa in the parlour as usual.

Flo had already said hello to Bunty and the fish and was curious to see who this Louis was.

She squealed when she saw him and, unable to resist the temptation, she rushed over and swept him off the sofa and into her arms. 'He's the most beautiful rabbit that I've ever seen,' she gushed, holding him tight.

'Help!' Louis screamed. He'd been half asleep when Flo grabbed him, and he wasn't best pleased at being hauled into a stranger's arms. 'Help!' he shouted again, only louder this time. 'I'm being kidnapped!'

'Don't be silly, Louis,' Eddie told him. 'This is Flo, and she's a friend of mine. She's just saying hello.'

'I suppose you can understand what the rabbit is saying?' Flo asked Eddie, not in the least bit surprised as she held on to the struggling Louis.

'I'm afraid so,' Eddie replied bashfully.

'Why did I bother asking.' Flo sighed, rolling her eyes, but also looking a bit impressed. 'What's he saying then?'

'He's demanding that I tell you to put him down as he doesn't like being handled, particularly by strangers,' Eddie told her with a big grin on his face.

'Oops,' Flo said apologetically, putting Louis quickly back

on the sofa. 'I'm sorry, Louis, I didn't mean to scare you. It's just that you look so . . . so . . .' she struggled to find the right word. 'So cuddly!' she said eventually. 'I couldn't help myself.'

'Cuddly, indeed.' Louis snorted in disgust, arranging himself comfortably on the sofa. 'Now, if you don't mind, tell her I want to be alone.'

They were all leaving anyway as Aunt Budge had planned a trip. 'I want to show you my new car,' she told them proudly. 'I'm afraid my old beauty will have to go into retirement, although I'll still use it for very special occasions that require me to arrive in style. Whetstone isn't happy about it at all, as he loves that old motor. Anyway, I've bought a jolly little electric car,' she said, clapping her hands together. 'Perfect for these roads and good for the environment as well. So, how do you fancy a little spin into Hythe?' she suggested. 'I'll park up and then we can catch the train.'

'The train?' Eddie asked. 'Where are we going? London?'

'No, dear,' Aunt Budge replied. 'Somewhere far more interesting. Dungeness.'

CHAPTER FIFTEEN

The Romney, Hythe & Dymchurch Railway is no ordinary railway. Oh no. In fact, it is unique, and people from all over the world visit it just to travel from Hythe to Dungeness on this remarkable little train.

As they drove to the station in Aunt Budge's new electric car, she chatted about the railway non-stop. 'The carriages, or should I say coaches, of the train are miniature and yet they're roomy enough to sit quite comfortably in,' she enthused. 'But my favourites are the beautiful steam locomotives, also in miniature, that pull them.'

'Is it like a toy train?' Flo asked, trying to picture this miniature railway.

'Dear me, no,' Aunt Budge said, laughing. 'They're a lot bigger than that. Why there's even a little buffet car, and to use it you have to hop off at one of the stations and then stay in the buffet car and enjoy your drink until the train pulls into the next station when you can get off and return to your original coach.'

'Aunt Budge, mind that pheasant,' Eddie shouted suddenly, pointing at a dozy bird ambling casually across the road in front of the car.

'Don't worry dear, I've seen it,' Aunt Budge replied calmly, slowing down a little to let it pass. 'Such stupid birds,' she tutted. 'No road sense at all. You should have a word with them, Eddie, and instruct them in road safety.'

They soon arrived at Hythe, parked up, went inside the booking hall and bought three tickets. When Eddie and Flo set eyes on the train, they both thought it was unbelievable, and immediately they set about excitedly taking photos on their phones of each other standing next to the engine.

'Smile!' Aunt Budge shouted, holding her phone up so she could take a selfie of all three of them. 'Say cheese.'

Bunty, sitting in Eddie's shirt pocket, was only too happy to oblige and gave her biggest grin.

'How long does it take to get to Dungeness, Aunt Budge?' Eddie asked once they'd boarded the train and were all settled in. 'And can we swap carriages if we want to?'

'The journey takes approximately one hour and fifteen

minutes,' she replied. 'And I don't see the point of swapping around as we're perfectly suited where we are.'

'But can we visit the buffet?'

'Of course you can. But you know the rules about hopping on and off.'

Eddie and Flo couldn't wait to see the buffet car and promised Aunt Budge they'd do as she'd said.

'Oh, and by the way,' she added, passing a bag of boiled sweets around, 'you keep forgetting that these are called coaches and not carriages. Such information might come in handy should you find yourselves sitting next to somebody at a dinner party who works on the railways.'

Eddie and Flo doubted that they'd ever find themselves in that situation, but they appreciated the information, nevertheless.

'I like this little train,' panted Butch excitedly. He was standing on Flo's knee so he could look out of the window. 'They welcome dogs on board, not like some people I could mention – that bus driver, for instance.' And he growled as he recalled the time the driver of the number 10 bus had accused him of doing a wee on the stairs, which, of course, he hadn't. 'One day I'll have my revenge,' he threatened, baring his teeth and growling some more.

The sudden sound of coach doors slamming and a loud whistle signalled that the train was about to leave the station, and Eddie, instantly excited, felt an explosion of butterflies in his tummy.

'We're off,' Aunt Budge announced happily as the train slowly drew out of the station. There were a few people on the platform taking photos, and some of them were waving, so Eddie and Flo waved back. Even Aunt Budge joined in, and gave the smiling people on the platform a regal little wave, while Bunty, who was sitting on Eddie's shoulder and who loved waving, was giving it her all.

Once they got going, the noise of the wind rushing by through the open windows combined with the clatter of the wheels on the track and the occasional hoot of the train's whistle, made it all quite noisy.

'Would you mind closing the window a little?' Aunt Budge shouted.

'Pardon?' Eddie shouted back over the noise.

'I said would you mind closing the window a little, as I've only just had my hair done and I feel the wind is doing it no good. I'd hate to arrive looking as if I had a bird's nest on my head. My hairdresser would never forgive me.'

Eddie did as he was asked, but as he was closing the window he caught a whiff of steam from the engine, and with the wind in his face and the noise of the wheels, he was transported to another time and thought that this was the best train in the world.

Once the train stopped at St Mary's Bay station, Eddie and Flo jumped off and ran to the buffet car. It was as small as the other coaches with a little seating area at one end and a man behind a counter at the other selling drinks and crisps. They bought two orange drinks for themselves and a bottle of water for Aunt Budge, which they gave her when they got off and returned to their coach at the New Romney stop.

'Most considerate,' she said, taking a sip before pouring some out into the little plastic bowl Eddie had brought with him so Butch could also have a drink.

'Right on time,' Aunt Budge announced with a hint of pride in her voice, checking her watch as they pulled into Dungeness Station, the last stop on the line. 'Such a reliable service,' she congratulated the guard as he helped them off the train. 'The big rail networks could certainly learn a lot from you.'

CHAPTER SIXTEEN

The first thing they noticed when they left the station was the power station. 'What's that thing?' Flo asked.

'It's the nuclear power plant,' Aunt Budge told her. 'Not particularly pretty, but strangely, it seems to add to the environment.'

'Dungeness is a strange place,' Flo remarked as they walked towards the lighthouse. 'It's so wild.'

'I've seen places like this in Western movies,' Butch said, sniffing the ground suspiciously. 'We'd better watch out for cattle rustlers and bandits.'

'I read that they call Dungeness, "England's desert",' Eddie said, 'but I can't see any camels.'

'That's because it's not a desert,' Aunt Budge explained. 'Whoever thought that up was quite mistaken. Now, who fancies a trip up the lighthouse?'

The lighthouse was now a museum, and it was quite a climb up to the lamp room at the very top. Eddie and Flo were a bit out of breath when they got there, but Aunt Budge wasn't bothered in the least. 'Such good exercise,' she commented. 'Now, come and look at the view – it's magnificent.'

As it was a clear day, Eddie and Flo could see right across the English Channel to the coastline of France.

'Cool,' was all they could think of saying as, stunned into silence, they gazed at the view.

Flo bought three ice creams from the café. She insisted that she pay as she wanted to try out her English notes that she'd exchanged her savings for at the bank in Amsterdam. 'They're so slippery and shiny,' she said, holding up a five-pound note. 'Not at all like real money.'

They sat for a while eating their ice creams and watching Butch tiptoe around the shingle warily. Eddie broke the end of his cone off and, scooping up a piece of ice cream, he handed it to Bunty.

'I really shouldn't,' she said, grabbing the tiny cone quickly with both paws. 'But as it's a rare treat, it would be a bad show to refuse.'

'Just don't get it down my shirt,' Eddie warned, laughing as he watched her close her eyes and take a lick with an expression of sheer joy on her face.

After they'd finished their ice creams, Aunt Budge suggested a walk.

'Do us good, a nice long walk,' she said, rubbing her hands together. 'I have come prepared, after all.' She certainly had, as, apart from a pair of stout walking boots that she had on her feet and thick white socks, she was also wearing a tartan cloak and a man's deerstalker hat, which she wore at a jaunty angle.

'Shall we go then?' she said, pointing the cane she was carrying in the direction of the road. 'We'll go as far as Prospect Cottage and then turn back.'

As they walked down the road, Eddie and Flo struggling to match Aunt Budge's marching pace as she shouted, 'Keep up, keep up,' they noticed a black van approaching. The exhaust was belching out thick black smoke and the van spluttered and lurched, making a terrible racket.

'Good heavens,' Aunt Budge exclaimed as the van slowly crawled past them until with one final shudder and a loud bang from the exhaust, it came to a shuddering halt.

A weird little man in a dirty black suit climbed out of the driver's seat. It was Dennis Rancid, and by the sounds of his cursing and swearing he wasn't very happy, and nor was Demonica, who was yelling instructions from inside the van.

'It's the exhaust,' Dennis shouted to his sister. 'And the back doors have flung open again.'

'Well, they wouldn't if you tied the handles together, would they?' Demonica shouted back. 'Just get this heap started, will you, and let's get out of here.'

Dennis kicked the wheel of the van and muttered something that made Aunt Budge frown. Then, turning to her, he had the barefaced cheek to say, 'Instead of just standing there gawping, you could make yourself useful, you old bat, and give us a push.'

Aunt Budge looked at him as if she'd just stepped in something very unpleasant. 'The only push I'd give you would be straight into the nearest canal,' she replied, icily calm. 'And if I were you, which thankfully I'm not, I'd abandon that so-called vehicle and walk.'

'You wanna watch your mouth, lady,' Dennis threatened. 'Or else.'

'Or else what?' Aunt Budge demanded haughtily.

'Or else I might just beat those kids up and nick your handbag,' Dennis snarled.

'Just try it,' Eddie warned him in what he thought was his

'tough voice,' stepping in front of Aunt Budge.

Flo quickly joined in. 'Who are you going to beat up?' she asked Dennis, clenching her fists. 'If you want a fight then you've got one, although you know you'll lose.'

Dennis leant against the van and laughed and laughed and laughed.

'Oh, he finds it funny, does he?' Bunty said angrily as she popped out of Eddie's shirt pocket. 'Let me at him.'

'What's going on out there?' Demonica screeched from inside the van. 'Why the hold-up?'

'I'm being threatened by a pensioner and two snotty kids', he sneered nastily. 'But I'm going to teach them a lesson,' he added, rolling up the sleeves of his grubby jacket.

Butch, who hadn't trusted Dennis from the moment he saw him, decided enough was enough and that now was the time for action. Charging at Dennis, he made one almighty leap and bit him, right in an extremely sensitive area.

'OWWWWW!' Dennis roared, as he fell to his knees. 'He got me right in the goolies.'

'Language, please,' Aunt Budge reprimanded him. 'Serves you jolly well right. Now, come along children, we have a train to catch.'

'Not so fast,' Dennis snarled angrily. 'You ain't going anywhere, not until I've dealt with that dog.' Pulling a heavy metal bar out from the back of the van he walked slowly towards them, waving it about menacingly.

Butch growled and Eddie, quickly picking him up, shouted, 'You keep away from my dog!'

Just then, a motorbike that had been coming down the road skidded to a halt and pulled up next to them.

'Oh dear,' Aunt Budge moaned. 'More trouble.'

The rider got off the bike, and when she removed her helmet they were surprised and delighted to see that it was none other than Miss Schmidt. Dennis stopped short in the middle of the road, unsure now of what to do.

'Miss Schmidt,' Aunt Budge gasped. 'What on earth are you doing on that motorbike?'

'I'm taking it for a test drive,' she replied. 'I'm thinking of getting one as I miss my old motorbike. Don't forget,' she reminded Aunt Budge, 'I used to be a stunt rider on the Wall of Death at the fairground. Now tell me something, why is this angry little man holding a metal bar?'

'He's threatening to do something to Butch, that's why,' Eddie told her.

'Is he now,' Miss Schmidt replied, striding over to Dennis and calmly taking the bar out of his hand. 'I'll have that,' she said as Dennis stood there speechless. 'Now then, could you explain to me why you are being so aggressive?'

Dennis gaped open-mouthed at her. This was clearly not a woman to be messed with.

'Well, I just asked them politely to help me push my van,' he spluttered nervously. 'It's broken down, you see, and then, well, they were very rude and that rat of a dog attacked me.'

Miss Schmidt stared at him with steely eyes. 'I don't believe you,' she replied bluntly. 'In fact, if I was asked to sum up your character, I'd say that you were a bully and a coward who's never heard of deodorant.'

Dennis was speechless, and Demonica, listening from inside the van, decided that it was best to remain quiet in case this woman started on her.

'Now, I'm going to escort my employer and the children to the station, and I don't want another peep out of you. Understand?'

Dennis gulped. He couldn't answer as his mouth had gone dry.

'Did you hear me?' Miss Schmidt demanded, tapping her foot angrily.

Dennis nodded furiously to show that he'd heard her and had fully understood.

'Good,' she said.

Eddie and Flo laughed all the way back to the station as Butch marched proudly ahead with his head held high. 'No bandit is going to threaten my comrades,' he boasted in his Western-movie Mexican-bandit accent. 'I bite to keeeel.'

'Oh dear, what an experience,' Aunt Budge said to Miss Schmidt as she wheeled the motorbike alongside. 'What an absolute rotter of a man he was. And as for Butch biting him in the you-know-whats, well, I haven't seen anything like it since one of Her Majesty's corgis bit dear old Giddy Livermore on the ankle at a garden party.'

'Fancy Miss Schmidt being a stunt rider,' Eddie said to Flo, full of admiration that she'd once ridden the Wall of Death at the fairground.

Flo nodded in agreement. 'Cool,' she said. 'Super cool.'

Dennis watched them as they walked down the road. His

face twisted in a combination of anger and pure hatred. 'They haven't seen the last of me,' he muttered darkly to himself. 'I'll get them, and that little dog too.'

CHAPTER SEVENTEEN

'**O**h, the pain! Just look at my poor foot,' Demonica moaned, kicking her shoe off and holding her foot up for her brother to inspect. 'You can actually see the corn on my big toe throbbing. Look at it,' she whined, pointing at her toe.

'Ugh, you've got the ugliest feet on the planet,' Dennis replied, screwing his face up. 'As well as the largest and the smelliest, and that big toe looks just like a clown's nose. Put it away, will you?'

After the van had refused to start, they'd had no choice but to push it all the way home.

'Well, if we had decent transport my feet wouldn't be in this state,' she grumbled. 'I'm not cut out for pushing vans. We'll just have to get a new one.'

'And where are we going to find the money for a new van?' Dennis asked her. 'Drop into our local friendly neighbourhood bank and ask to borrow some cash? Oh yes, I'm sure they'd loan it to us in a heartbeat,' he added sarcastically.

'Well, nick a van then,' she said, rubbing her big toe. 'After all, you're the big, brave, fearless criminal aren't you? Just help yourself, as I'm sure nobody would dare stop a tough nut like you. Why, look at how you dealt with that band of yobs on the road,' she went on slyly. 'You were ready to beat the lot of them up. What a brave brother I have.'

'Well, there were four against one, not to mention that dog,' Dennis protested. 'It wasn't fair, I was outnumbered.'

'We're talking about an old woman and a couple of kids here,' Demonica said witheringly. 'And as for that woman on the motorbike, she should've been a pushover to deal with.'

'A pushover to deal with?!' Dennis almost screeched as he raised his voice in disbelief. 'Did you see her? She bent my crowbar as easily as if it was a piece of toffee! Why didn't *you* get out of the van and do something instead of just sitting there, if you thought that giant of a woman was such a pushover?'

Demonica simply snorted by way of reply.

'What about that dog? It bit me,' he winced. 'I'm still sore, and I bet I'm bruised.'

'I don't wish to know,' Demonica sniffed, wrinkling her nose up in disgust and turning away from her brother. 'And can you kindly stop fiddling with yourself in front of a lady!'

Dennis looked around himself. 'I can't see any lady,' he told her with a wicked grin on his face. 'Only you, picking away at your size-ten foot.'

Demonica threw her shoe at him. 'Why don't you go and see if you can start the stove up, you big buffoon,' she demanded. 'There's a bag full of shopping that we've just paid good money for that needs to be cooked.'

Dennis slunk off into the kitchen to have a look at the ancient kitchen range, and after studying it for a while, announced that he'd be able to get it up and running in no time.

'There's some old birds' nests in here,' he said prodding a stick into a tangle of twigs, moss and feathers inside the oven.

'Well, that will come in handy if we ever open up as a bird sanctuary,' his sister replied, moaning as she continued to rub her big toe. 'Hurry up and get it working so we can boil the kettle for some tea. That's if there is such a thing as a kettle in this rat trap of a hovel.'

There was a kettle, as it happened – old and a bit rusty, but still serviceable and there were also a few battered pans as well as the big iron frying pan that Demonica had thrown at Dennis.

'Here, I've found that frying pan you flung at me,' he exclaimed delightedly. 'Now when I get this fire going—'

'Don't you mean if?' his sister interrupted him.

'No, I mean *when* I get it going. I am an expert at starting fires, after all,' he boasted. 'I could fry them kippers we bought and now that the dirty water in the tap is running clear we could have a cup of tea as well.'

'If you manage that, dear brother,' Demonica replied, sighing at the thought of tea and fried kippers, 'I promise I'll never put chewing gum in your hair again or itching powder in your underpants.'

The range was more difficult to get going than Dennis thought. He'd cleared out the rubble, but left the twigs and the birds' nests inside as tinder. He thought that he'd cracked it, but it refused to light.

'I know what I'll do,' Dennis chuckled, having just had a brainwave. 'There's a can of petrol in the van, that should do the job. I'll go and fetch it.'

'Are you sure about this?' Demonica asked doubtfully, as she watched him lashing petrol into the stove. 'It looks dangerous to me, and I'm sure there's no need to use the whole can, a tiny drop would be enough.'

'Stop moaning and hand me those matches,' Dennis told her. 'I know what I'm doing. Don't forget, I used to be in the Scouts.'

'Yes, for two days,' Demonica reminded him. 'Until you burnt the Scout hut down.'

'Well, at least I got my Firefighter proficiency badge,' he said with a smile as he struck a match and threw it into the stove. 'Any minute now, we're going to have a roaring—'

But he never got to finish what he was saying as there was a blinding flash of light followed by a deafening *BOOM!!!* that shook the house and brought half of the ceiling down, sending both Dennis and Demonica flying.

They sat in the debris, covered from head to toe in soot, in stunned silence. Dennis's hair was standing on end, and neither of them could hear a thing as their ears were ringing loudly from the noise of the explosion.

Eventually Dennis gave a weak little smile and, swallowing hard, he said nervously, 'At least we can look on the bright side.'

'And what's that?' Demonica moaned, rubbing her head as a large piece of the ceiling fell down next to her.

'The stove's on fire.' He grinned happily. 'Shall I make us a nice cup of tea?'

CHAPTER EIGHTEEN

Over the next few days, Eddie and Flo set about exploring on Aunt Budge's electric bicycles. They bought ice cream in Dymchurch and visited the amusement park, where they were surprised to find Miss Schmidt enjoying herself on the dodgems.

'I often pop in here when I get the chance,' she confessed. 'I find the dodgems extremely exciting.'

'Don't you miss riding your motorbike in the fairground?' Flo asked, picking at a great ball of sticky candyfloss. 'It must have been really thrilling.'

'Yes, I suppose it was,' Miss Schmidt agreed. 'I rode the Wall of Death ten times a day, and then in the evening they put a rubber mermaid's tail on me and a long blonde wig and I swam around in a tank of water as "Marina the Mermaid: Half-Fish Half-Woman, the Most Amazing Spectacle in the World", at least that's what it said on the billboard outside the tent,' she said, making a noise that might have been a tiny laugh.

They passed a man holding a long-handled hammer who was shouting, 'Test your strength, hit the bell and win a lovely prize!'

'Go on, Miss Schmidt, why don't you have a try?' Eddie said. 'After the way you bent that metal bar, I bet you'd hit that bell easily.'

The man with the hammer looked horrified as he realised that Miss Schmidt was approaching.

'No chance,' he protested, holding his arm out as if to keep Miss Schmidt away. 'Oh no, you're not having a go. Not after the last time when you didn't just hit the bell, you managed to knock it straight off the top of the stand and send it flying through the roof of the hoopla stall. You're banned for life,' he added angrily.

'But you can't just ban someone because they're strong,' Eddie told the man reasonably.

'That's right,' Flo agreed. 'You are inviting people to test their strength, after all.'

'Well, there's strength and there's strength,' the man argued, and she's got super strength. What are you?' he asked Miss Schmidt. 'A wrestler or something?'

'I wrestled an alligator once when I worked in the movies,' she informed him haughtily. 'But I'm better known as the finest cook in Bavaria. Now, come along children,' she said, stalking off. 'There are far more interesting attractions to be found in Kent than this silly Test Your Strength contraption.' And she marched smartly off with Eddie and Flo trying to keep up behind her.

Indeed, there certainly were lots more interesting things to do. Aunt Budge drove them in her little car to visit Dover Castle and to see the world-famous white cliffs. Butch stayed at home with Whetstone and as Aunt Budge was driving herself, Whetstone didn't have much to do, so the pair of them spent a lot of time in Whetstone's room watching old cowboy films, which they both loved.

Louis lay on the sofa as usual, planning his return to the

French stage and cinema. 'I might do a musical comedy,' he told himself. 'Or would that destroy my reputation as a serious actor? Such problems.'

The fish were discussing what to put in their memoirs. 'It's going to be a scorcher,' Dan bragged to Bunty. 'An international bestseller.' He was hanging over the side of the tank so he could talk to Bunty, who was sitting on a pack of playing cards trying to ignore a bowl of fruit nearby.

Jake came up out of the water to join his brother. 'We're going to name names,' he told her excitedly. 'No holds barred.'

'You'd better be careful what you write,' Bunty replied, eyeing up a grape that was fast becoming irresistible. 'You might end up in court.'

'Well, we ain't scared of no court,' Jake boasted. 'And anyway, where is it? Hampton Court? Tennis court, royal court, Earl's Court?'

'Caught in a net?' Dan said, joining in this game of 'Name that Court'. 'Caught a cold? Caught a ball?'

Bunty was ignoring them, nibbling furiously on a large chunk of grape. 'Bliss,' she murmured as she munched away contentedly.

*

One morning Aunt Budge took Eddie and Flo to Canterbury Cathedral and they all had tea with Aunt Budge's old friend, who had recently retired as the Dean of the Cathedral. In a garden surrounded by an ancient wall the Dean kept a variety of animals – pigs, rabbits, hens and a very noisy rooster.

'Do stop,' the Dean asked the rooster politely as the bird belted out yet another *cock-a-doodle-doo*. 'We're trying to have our tea in peace.'

The rooster tilted his head to one side, shook his tail feathers indignantly and strode off towards the hens.

'Oh dear,' the Dean said, blowing on his cup of tea to cool it down. 'I hope I haven't offended him. He can be very touchy, you know.'

They visited the ancient town of Rye with its past history of smugglers and spent an afternoon at Port Lympne Wildlife Park, where Eddie had a very interesting conversation with a rhino.

But for Flo, the best thing ever was the picnic in an ancient bluebell wood. They sat in a part of the wood that was clear of the bluebells so they didn't crush any. Whetstone had brought a table and chairs, the table having been laid out for tea, complete with a tablecloth and Aunt Budge's china. The food was delicious, as always, with some of Miss Schmidt's little cakes and a selection of pastries and sandwiches, which she'd packed carefully in a hamper.

'Isn't this heavenly?' Aunt Budge sighed happily as Whetstone poured her tea into a bone-china cup. 'Sitting in a wood surrounded by bluebells having our tea. It really doesn't get any better.'

Flo and Eddie totally agreed with her, as it really was quite an unusual, not to mention, magical experience. Eddie had always believed that woods were mysterious places. Whenever he walked through a wood, he'd get the feeling that whatever lived there had suddenly stopped what they were doing until he had passed by. Even now, as he munched on a cake, Eddie couldn't help thinking that they were being quietly observed by someone or something.

Flo took lots of pictures to send to her family. She took some of Butch and Bunty sitting among the bluebells, and a particularly wonderful one of Louis stretched out on a log, sniffing a bluebell. Eddie took photos as well, sending them off to his dad to show him that they were having a good time.

After they'd finished their tea, Flo and Eddie offered to help

Whetstone clear the tea things away, but he wouldn't hear of it.

'It's my job,' he protested. 'And I have my way of doing things, but I appreciate the offer.'

'And I'm a very fortunate woman having Whetstone and Miss Schmidt to look after me,' Aunt Budge said. 'Even if they are a pair of miseries,' she added as an afterthought. 'Now let's have a little stroll before we go home, shall we?'

CHAPTER NINETEEN

'I needed that,' Dennis announced, leaning back in his chair and belching loudly. 'That was the best meal I've had in ages, even if the kippers did taste a little bit of petrol.'

Between them they'd polished off half a loaf of bread, three tins of beans, a pot of strawberry jam, two pairs of kippers, six bags of cheese-and-onion crisps and endless mugs of tea.

'I wish you'd find something to wear,' Demonica said disapprovingly as she rubbed a piece of bread around her plate to soak up the last of the baked-bean juice. 'It's just as well I've got a strong stomach as the sight of you in your dirty vest and underpants would put anyone off their food.'

They'd managed to boil a kettle of water and fill up the big stone sink so they could wash the soot off their faces. They'd also had to take their clothes off and beat them hard with a broom to get the soot out of them. They were now hanging up on a washing line outside, which is why Dennis was sitting in his underwear.

Demonica, not wishing to walk around in her underwear, had wandered upstairs to have a look in Old Molly Maggot's bedroom and had found a wardrobe full of old clothes. The moths had eaten most of them, but she'd managed to find some sort of dressing gown to wear that didn't have too many holes in it.

'Go upstairs and look for something to put on,' she told her brother, her face still streaked here and there with soot. 'There's men's clothes in the wardrobe as well as Molly Maggot's. They must've belonged to her husband, or then again, they could easily have been hers.'

'All right,' her brother said grumpily, getting up from the chair and going upstairs. 'Just to shut you up, I'll put something on. Although, I'll have you know that there's many who'd pay good money to see my body.'

'Yes,' Demonica replied. 'Like taxidermists and undertakers.'

She watched him climbing the stairs and shuddered. 'And pull those baggy underpants up. I don't want to be looking at your bum, especially after I've just eaten kippers and baked beans.'

She could hear him banging about upstairs as she went into the kitchen, carefully stepping over a beam that had fallen down from the ceiling following the explosion. The room stank of petrol, and there was still a small flame burning in the stove. She tried to open a window to let in some fresh air, but it was firmly sealed shut. So she flung a pan through it instead, smashing the glass.

'That's one way to open a window,' she muttered to herself as she picked her way around the floor. Then she stubbed her sore toe on something hard. She let out a yell, and bending down to investigate, she saw that it was a large book half-covered by the debris.

'This must've been hidden under the upstairs floorboards,' she concluded. 'But why would anyone hide a book?' she wondered aloud. 'Unless it was a person's diary!' Gleefully, she sat down with it on her knee. Reading other people's private diaries was a pastime that Demonica particularly enjoyed.

The book was bound with tape and its cover was stiff with age. Once she'd brushed away the years of soot and dust from the cover, she saw that there was an inscription in faded red lettering.

'*Spells, Incantations and Potions,*' it read, and on undoing the tape and opening the book, Demonica found something equally interesting written in spidery handwriting on the first page. 'This book belongs to Molly Maggot.'

'*Spells, Incantations and Potions*? So, she was a witch after all,' Demonica said out loud, her beady black eyes gleaming as she turned the pages, wondering what the many strange symbols and weird illustrations of plants and animals could mean. 'I wonder if she was a good witch or a bad one? I hope she was a bad one, a really truly rotten evil one,' she cackled. '*A spell to enchant*,' she read. 'Now that might come in handy, but I'm not sure about the *How to strike a neighbour's cow with the sickness spell*, not unless I have a row with a farmer.'

There was one spell, however, that really caught Demonica's eye: *A Spell to Retrieve the Smugglers' Treasure*. Now, that sounded extremely interesting, and immediately an image of a treasure chest stuffed full of crunchy uncut diamonds and gold coins flashed before her eyes.

She was so engrossed in the book that she didn't hear or see her brother coming down the stairs.

'Boo!' he shouted, causing Demonica to leap out of her chair with fright.

'What are you doing creeping up on me like that?' she shrieked angrily, clutching the book to her chest. 'Are you trying to kill me or something?'

'Well, the thought had crossed my mind,' he answered slyly, 'but what do you think of my new look?'

She stared at him in shock before bursting into a fit of uncontrollable giggles. 'You look ridiculous,' she screeched. 'I've seen better-dressed scarecrows.'

The more she laughed, the more Dennis silently fumed. He'd thought he looked quite dashing in his military jacket and jodhpurs. Okay, the riding boots that were far too big for him might possibly spoil the overall effect, but the three-cornered hat with the large, slightly battered red feather sticking out of the top he considered to be a real touch of class.

'Well, that's cheered me up no end,' she wheezed, sitting

down to get her breath back now that she'd managed to stop laughing. 'You look a right dork.'

'Well, I bet you some of these clothes are worth money,' he replied sulkily. 'There's loads of them upstairs, some of them I'd say are antiques that a museum would pay a fortune for.'

'Don't talk daft,' Demonica said dismissively. 'They're nothing but old rags. I'll show you something that'll bring the money rolling in.'

'What?' Dennis asked, still sulking.

'This!' she crowed triumphantly holding the book up. 'This is Old Molly Maggot's spell book.'

'Oh.'

'Is that all you can say? This book holds the secret of how we can get our hands on some treasure.'

'Stuff and nonsense.' Now it was Dennis's turn to scoff dismissively. 'Nothing more than a fairy tale. How can you believe such rubbish?'

'You won't be saying that when, thanks to this book, we uncover an absolute fortune in buried treasure,' she said greedily. 'Now, put the kettle on before the flame burns out on the range. I'll need a strong cup of tea as I study this book in great detail.'

CHAPTER TWENTY

'When is Stanley arriving?' Flo asked Eddie as they sat in the parlour waiting for a sudden burst of rain to stop. 'It'll be good to see him after so long. I miss him, and I can tell that Casey misses him too. I wish he'd pop over to Amsterdam to visit him sometime.'

In case you don't remember, Casey was the parrot that Eddie and Flo rescued from the evil Vera van Loon, and who now lived with Flo and her family.

'Well, Stanley said he'd be here before Easter,' Eddie told her. 'But you know what he's like, he could turn up at any time. Why, he might even be in Amsterdam right now.'

'Who is this Stanley?' Louis asked, slowly opening one eye to look at Eddie. He was lying on Flo's lap and feeling very sleepy as she stroked his back. 'Tell her to do behind the ears, will you?' he asked Eddie before closing his eye again and sighing contentedly.

'Louis just asked if you could do behind his ears,' Eddie told Flo, who laughed, no longer surprised when Eddie talked to animals.

'Mmmmmm,' Louis moaned, his back leg twitching as Flo tickled behind his ear. 'Heavenly,' he purred happily.

'And to answer your question, Louis,' Eddie continued. 'Stanley is a crow. I hand-reared him after he fell out of his nest in Stanley Park, but he's fully grown now, of course.'

'He must be a very famous bird if they named a park after him,' Louis murmured drowsily. 'Very famous indeed. Did they erect a statue to him as well?'

'No,' Eddie started to explain as he tried to keep a straight face. 'I named Stanley after the park, not the other way round.'

'Oh,' Louis replied, yawning. Now that he knew Stanley wasn't famous he'd lost interest.

'Two things,' Aunt Budge announced, bursting into the room and waving a letter. 'The first thing is this,' she said, sitting down. 'I've had the organiser of the village fête on the phone. Apparently, a local celebrity – who, quite frankly I've never heard of, but he came sixth in a singing competition on television – has had to pull out of opening their fête due to some filming commitment, and he wondered if I'd step in and do the honours instead. Well, of course, I had to say yes, even if I do find these things a little embarrassing. I suppose I'll have to wear gloves and a very large hat,' she added, sighing.

'What's the second thing?' Eddie asked.

'Oh yes. Now this is the best news ever,' Aunt Budge said excitedly, waving the letter again. 'Do you remember me telling you about Giddy Livermore? She's that old friend of mine who was nipped on the ankle by the Queen's corgi. Well, she's sent me this little note saying she's driving to France with her elder brother and wonders if she could pop in on her way to the Channel Tunnel to say hello. I haven't seen old Giddy in years, and I'm very fond of her, it'll be so nice to catch up.'

'Giddy?' Flo asked. 'That's a strange name.'

'Well, her real name is Griselda, such an appalling name to inflict on a young gal, don't you agree?' Aunt Budge said, pulling a face. 'Anyway, everyone has always called her Giddy, which suits her down to the ground as she's a lot of fun, and I'm sure you'll love her, although heaven knows how old her brother must be by now. She's arriving early tomorrow afternoon, so I must ask Miss Schmidt to cater for an extra two for lunch, not that she'll mind as she's a big fan of Giddy.'

'And what about this fête?' Eddie asked. 'Can we come?'

'Why, of course you must come,' Aunt Budge replied. 'And we must find you both something suitable to wear as the theme this year is Pirates and Smugglers.'

Eddie was all for it, but Flo wasn't that keen. 'Do we have to wear fancy dress?' she frowned. 'It's not very cool.'

'Nonsense,' Aunt Budge exclaimed. 'Everyone gets into the spirit and dresses up. It'll be fun, and there's a prize for the best costume. You'd make a lovely pirate, Flo. I'll get in touch with a theatrical costumier I know in London and have him send some things down.'

Flo still wasn't sure, but as Aunt Budge and Eddie seemed so enthusiastic, she gave in. 'Okay,' she said, shrugging her shoulders and laughing. 'A pirate it is, then. It's just a shame I didn't bring Casey – he could've sat on my shoulder.'

'I don't think the village is quite ready for Casey just yet,' Aunt Budge said with a wink. 'He might swear at the vicar. Now why don't you two go out? The rain has stopped and it's too nice a day to be sat indoors.'

CHAPTER TWENTY-ONE

I n Dungeness, however, the sun certainly wasn't shining on Wych Way. It was so well hidden behind the power station that the sun hardly got near it, and consequently the house was shrouded in a permanent shadowy gloom.

'This makes fascinating reading,' Demonica said as she slurped her mug of tea and studied the book that she had found. 'Especially the stuff about the buried treasure and, more importantly, the secret to getting my hands on it,' she added greedily.

'*Your* hands on it?' Dennis asked, raising his eyebrows. 'What happened to *our* hands?'

'I meant *our* hands,' Demonica replied, even though she didn't, for if there was any treasure to be found, then it was all going to be hers, right down to the very last teeny-weeny diamond. She had absolutely no intention of sharing the treasure with her brother, although she knew she might need his help in obtaining it, so for now she intended to keep Dennis on her side.

'Of course we'll share the treasure, brother darling,' she assured him with a sickly smile. 'Split right down the middle, fifty-fifty, but you'll have to help me.'

'Well, I ain't digging.' Dennis snorted grumpily. 'If there's digging to be done, we'll have to nick one of those mechanical digger things from a building site.'

'Which, of course, wouldn't draw any attention to us at all,' Demonica pointed out. 'And besides, according to this book there isn't any digging required. All it involves is a spell.'

When Dennis heard this, he couldn't help laughing. 'A spell?' he spluttered. 'Oh, come on, Demonica, aren't you a bit old for witches and wizards? That kind of stuff belongs in a kids' book.'

'Well, Old Molly Maggot was obviously a witch,' a red-faced Demonica said, defending herself. 'She was notorious in these parts. And if she wasn't a witch then why would she have this spell book? And why would she have hidden it? Answer that, smarty-pants.'

Dennis shook his head in disbelief. 'She was probably just some old woman who lived on her own, minding her own business until they wanted to pull her house down, and so she said she was a witch and would curse the builders if they came near, to scare them off.'

This was quite a reasonable speech for Dennis, and it took Demonica by surprise.

'No, there's more to it than that. Why else would she have so many broomsticks in the cupboard?'

'Maybe she liked cleaning,' Dennis replied. 'Some people do, you know. Can you think of another reason?'

'To fly on, you idiot,' she hissed. 'There's a recipe in here for flying ointment. Apparently you rub it on the broom, chant a few spells and then the broom will fly. I've just got to find the right herbs to make the potion.'

Dennis stared at her open-mouthed. 'I've heard it all now. Flying broomsticks?' he exclaimed. 'Well, if this Molly Maggot was such a hotshot witch, why didn't she just cast a few spells, get the treasure and fly out of this hellhole? What stopped her? Tell me that, Miss Smarty-Knickers.'

'Well, I don't know. Maybe she couldn't find the right items needed for the spell to open up the portal.'

'The what?'

'The portal. It's a magic doorway that leads to the treasure.'

'And where exactly is this buried treasure?'

'Inside an ancient hill called Ollington Knoll,' Demonica replied. 'We'll have to pay it a little visit.'

CHAPTER TWENTY-TWO

Giddy arrived the next afternoon right on the dot of midday. She was driving a bright-red sports car with her brother in the passenger seat, and she was honking the horn loudly and repeatedly as she sped down the drive towards the cottage to let everyone know she was coming.

'Here they are,' Aunt Budge shouted excitedly, rushing out of the house to greet them as the car pulled up outside.

'Budge!' Giddy roared, leaping out of the car and throwing her arms round Aunt Budge in a bear hug. She was a big lady, and Eddie noticed that the coat she was wearing was exactly the same colour as her car. Aunt Budge and Giddy clung on to each other, tears of joy streaming down both their faces as they leapt up and down, squealing happily like a couple of teenagers who'd just won tickets to see their favourite band.

'Oi, what about me?' Giddy's brother, who was still sitting

in the car shouted. 'Come and give me a hand getting out of this thing.'

'I'm coming, Jacob,' Giddy said, laughing loudly. 'He's older than time, you know, and needs a little help to get out of my car.'

'Well, if you drove something sensible, I wouldn't need help,' Jacob replied as Giddy ran round the car to help her brother.

The bright-red sports car was very low to the ground, and getting Jacob out took a lot of tugging and pulling.

'Mind my arm, will you,' he moaned grumpily as Giddy grabbed hold of him. 'And don't drag me like that. I'm not a bag of coal.'

Eventually Giddy got him out of the car, and Eddie could see that he was a very old man indeed.

'Jacob,' Aunt Budge gushed, giving the frail old man a gentle hug. 'How lovely to see you after all this time. Come and meet my family, and then we'll get you into the house.'

The introductions were made, with Giddy declaring that Butch was the most adorable little dog she'd ever set eyes on. She swept him up into her arms and gave him a kiss. Butch was a sucker for flattery, and he responded by wagging his tail excitedly and giving her face a lick.

'Come on then,' Aunt Budge said. 'Let's go inside.'

'Wait a bit, Budge,' Jacob told her, leaning on his walking stick and looking up at the cottage. 'I'd like to take a good look at the old place first, if you don't mind, that is.'

Giddy and Aunt Budge agreed and, joining him, they held hands and stood in silence, remembering a time long ago when they were very young and the world was different.

'Let's go inside,' Flo whispered to Eddie. 'The old folks are remembering.'

Once inside, there was endless chatter. Giddy was very loud and laughed a lot and occasionally both she and Aunt Budge would touch on a subject that had them both in tears and hugging again.

Jacob sat in a big armchair drinking his tea, nodding his head in agreement and smiling to himself as he remembered the old stories that Aunt Budge was recounting.

'How did you all meet?' Flo asked, when she could get a word in edgeways. 'I'd love to know.'

'Well,' Aunt Budge said, wiping her eyes. 'It's a long story, quite sad in places, but it does have a happy ending; at least I think it does.'

'Of course it does,' Giddy interrupted. 'Look at us now compared to when we were kids. Who'd have thought back then that we'd have done so well.'

'Indeed,' Aunt Budge replied and, sitting back in her chair, she began to tell the story of how they all met.

CHAPTER TWENTY-THREE

'As I've already told you,' Aunt Budge said to Eddie and Flo, 'I wasn't born rich – quite the opposite, in fact, as my family were very poor.'

'Same here,' Giddy agreed. 'We arrived from Trinidad to a cold and miserable London. People weren't very friendly towards us, and finding somewhere to live wasn't easy. In the end, all eight of us lived in the most terrible room.'

'A slum,' Jacob added, frowning. 'Not fit for cattle.'

'So,' Aunt Budge went on, 'in those days, there was a scheme that gave poor children who couldn't afford a holiday the chance to go on one in the countryside for a few weeks.'

'And this was it,' Giddy shouted triumphantly. 'Fresh air, good food and sunshine in this beautiful cottage that was run by a kind couple called Mr and Mrs Shepherd.'

'And they were like shepherds, when you think about it,'

Aunt Budge said. 'Keeping an eye on their flock of children.'

'Now then,' Giddy announced, clapping her hands together. 'Perhaps you'd like to hear my story.'

'Oh dear,' Jacob moaned. 'It's going to be a long afternoon.'

Ignoring her brother, she started to tell her tale.

'I was always making clothes for my doll out of any old scraps of material I could find,' she said. 'I made a doll, complete with a dress sewn from an old tea towel, for your Aunt Budge.'

'So you did,' Aunt Budge agreed. 'I've still got it.'

'No!' Giddy gasped. 'After all these years, you've still got that doll? Where is it?'

'Upstairs in my bedroom where she belongs. You made it for me in this very house, so it's only fitting that she should return home. She's very precious to me.'

This made Giddy cry, and Aunt Budge wasn't long in joining her, and together they clutched each other's hands and sobbed.

'Give it up,' Jacob growled. 'You're making a show of yourselves.'

'Anyway,' Giddy said, wiping her eyes and sniffing. 'I progressed from dolls to clothes, and by the time I was nineteen I'd managed to rent a little shop, and I started to sell the dresses I'd made. Do you remember that shop, Jacob?'

she added, turning to her brother.

'Course I do,' he muttered. 'I decorated it for you, didn't I?'

'Well, people liked my designs and I soon sold out. And as I couldn't keep up with the demand, I hired some machinists, and the next thing I knew, I had a business.'

'And then an empire,' Aunt Budge added. 'Don't be modest, Giddy, you've worked extremely hard and deserve your success.'

'How silly of me,' Flo suddenly exclaimed. 'You're Giddy from the "Giddy Up" fashion range. They sell your clothes in the big department store in Amsterdam. I love your clothes as they're so bright and colourful.'

'Thank you, sweetheart,' Giddy replied, blowing Flo a kiss. 'I love colour. I can't stand those dull shades of grey and brown, and as for that awful taupe . . .' She shuddered. 'Well, that's just plain revolting. I'll make you something nice and bright and perhaps a waistcoat for Eddie and a little coat for this sweet dog.'

Eddie wasn't sure about a waistcoat, but Flo seemed delighted, and as for Butch, well, he was in his element. Apart from his favourite poncho, he wasn't that keen on wearing coats, but he was so taken with Giddy that if she'd suggested he wore a suit of doggie armour, he'd have happily agreed.

'Now, can we have a look at the upstairs?' Giddy asked Aunt Budge. 'I'd love to see our old room. Are you coming, Jacob?'

'I'll stay here, if you don't mind,' he said. 'I'm not too good on stairs these days. I'll watch the kids and tell them a bit about *my* story.'

Aunt Budge and Giddy laughed. 'I think it's you the kids should be watching,' Giddy told him, and chattering away like two budgies they made their way upstairs.

When Jacob was young, back home in Trinidad, he told them, he'd worked as a trainee gardener. He remembered picking pomegranates straight off the tree, and the beauty of the scarlet chaconia flowers. It was always warm and sunny in Trinidad, and so arriving at Tilbury Docks on a rainy morning after a long boat voyage had come as a bit of a shock. Eventually he'd found a job keeping the parks tidy, but when his little sister Giddy went off to stay in Kent, he answered a job advert for a gardener not far from the cottage so he could stay close to her.

'I liked it so much that I stayed for quite some time,' he explained. 'It's a beautiful part of the country – the garden of England they call it, although if they build any more housing estates down here and litter good arable land with solar panels, it won't be a garden any more,' he said, suddenly angry. 'It's a crying shame the way they're carving up the countryside, and I don't hold with it.'

He sat quietly for a moment, staring into space as he thought about the Kent of his youth, before speaking again. 'Have you managed to have a good look around since you got here?' he asked. 'Been up the Knoll yet?'

'The what?' Eddie replied. 'What's a knoll?'

'It's a hill,' he explained. 'A very special hill, and it's even older than me.' Jacob chortled. 'It's been home to many things in its time – a pagan temple, a Roman navigation beacon, a look-out during both the Napoleonic Wars as well as the Second World War, and it was a favourite of smugglers who could signal to their comrades at Dymchurch. You should pay it a visit, but be careful,' he warned, wagging a finger; 'all isn't what it seems.'

'Why?' Eddie and Flo asked at the same time, curious as to what might be there.

'There are lots of legends surrounding that old knoll,' he said, lowering his voice. 'Some say there's two entrances; one leads to Faerie-land, but the other one is the Gate of Hell, the entrance to what some call the Underland. Buried deep inside the Knoll is a fortune in smugglers' treasure. But it's guarded by the ghosts of thirteen drowned pirates.'

'Oh, that's just silly,' Flo declared dismissively in her usual blunt manner. 'There's no such thing as fairies or ghosts.'

'Sssh,' Jacob warned, putting his finger to his lips and glancing around the room. 'Be careful what you say. They might hear you.'

'I doubt it,' Flo replied. 'They're upstairs.'

'Not Budge and Giddy,' Jacob told her. 'I'm talking about the little people, there's lots of them about in the woods, as well as on the Marshes, and they don't take kindly to anyone speaking ill of them.'

Flo still wasn't convinced, but secretly, and just to be on the safe side, she'd be careful what she said about fairies in future.

'Why hasn't the Knoll been excavated?' Eddie asked. 'To see if there really is any buried treasure?'

'Because, over the centuries, anyone who has tried to dig up the Knoll hasn't lasted very long. Those that have been foolish enough to try have always been found dead in the morning. The Knoll is best respected and left untouched,' Jacob warned.

'Really?' Flo asked, still not quite believing any of this. 'What did they die of?'

'Fright,' Jacob replied in a hushed voice. 'There was no other explanation for it – they died of sheer fright.'

CHAPTER TWENTY-FOUR

Across the Marshes in the ramshackle house behind the power station in Dungeness, there had also been talk of buried treasure. Since Demonica had found that spell book of Old Molly Maggot's and read about the legend of the buried treasure and, more importantly, how she could get hold of it, she'd talked of nothing else. She was desperate to see what the Knoll looked like, and roping Dennis in to drive the battered old van that he'd managed to repair, they were finally setting out for Ollington.

Unfortunately for them, to reach the Knoll you have to climb a very steep hill and, of course, their old van couldn't quite manage the climb and did what it usually did – it broke down, meaning that Demonica and Dennis had to get out and push it the rest of the way.

They parked the van outside a gate that opened on to a big field full of sheep and lambs. They could barely speak as they staggered into the field and fell exhausted on to the grass.

'That van,' Demonica gasped, struggling to breathe, 'will be the death of me. It'll have to go.'

'Well, if that's the case,' Dennis replied, panting like an old bloodhound, 'it seems like a good enough reason to keep it.'

'Oh, why wasn't I born an orphan?' Demonica moaned to herself. 'Instead of being stuck with this hateful halfwit?'

They lay on the grass, puffing and blowing like two fish out of water gasping for air, until eventually they felt able to get up and go in search of the Knoll. This didn't take them very long as it was staring them straight in the face.

'Is that it?' Dennis wasn't impressed. He'd expected something bigger and more mysterious. 'It's just an ordinary old hill with a load of nettles on top, nothing special about that.'

'But it's what's inside that counts,' Demonica reminded him, licking her lips greedily. 'A fortune in smugglers' treasure. Let's climb it.'

Dennis moaned about there being too many bends to navigate and how he was sick of climbing, but Demonica wasn't listening to him. She was so eager to see what was up there that she practically raced to the top.

'Not much up here of any interest,' she shouted down to her brother, who was slowly making his way up behind her, and who had now found himself caught in a large bed of nettles.

'Ow! Ow! Ow!' he squealed as each one stung him.

'Mind the nettles,' Demonica shouted, smirking.

'I'm covered in nettle stings,' Dennis said when he finally made it to the top. 'And what do I find when I get up here? Nothing. That's what.'

'Well, the view's not bad,' Demonica said, wincing in the sunlight. 'If you like that sort of thing.'

'I'm not interested in views,' Dennis said irritably, scratching the back of his hand. 'Any sign of your so-called, highly-unlikely-to-appear, magical portal?'

'There's a few badger holes dotted around the side,' Demonica replied, leaning over to get a better look. 'Maybe one of those will turn into the portal.'

'Don't talk daft, woman.' Dennis was getting tired of what he considered to be a load of old nonsense. His legs were aching from pushing the van up the hill and then having to climb the Knoll (which really is not that steep). He was covered in nettle stings and the itching was driving him crazy, plus he was starving and wanted nothing more than to sit down in a nice café with a big plate of meat pie and peas with chips and gravy, all washed down with a mug of strong tea, and the racing page of the newspaper propped up against the sauce bottle so he could eat and read at the same time. And yet here he was, stuck on top of a hill, chasing his sister's ridiculous dreams.

'Can you please stop scratching, you're like a mangey old dog with fleas,' Demonica complained. 'You're also ruining my concentration as I try to feel the Vibes.'

This made Dennis laugh. 'The what?' he sniggered, forgetting for a moment that he was annoyed with her because she hadn't shown him any sympathy over his nettle stings.

'The Vibes,' Demonica replied grandly. 'You wouldn't understand such things.' And throwing her head back, she raised up her arms as if to embrace the sky. 'Listen to me, oh spirits of the Knoll,' she wailed. 'As well as all you fairies . . . and . . . erm . . .' She struggled to find a suitable word and, unable to think of one, she settled for, 'and the rest of you.'

In her imagination she saw herself as a powerful sorceress: her long, flowing hair the colour of a raven's wing blowing in the wind, with a black velvet cloak flapping behind her as the skies turned dark and the storm that she was conjuring up drew nearer.

'Speak to ME,' she howled, causing Dennis to leap out of his skin. He was now sitting on the grass a short distance away from her, and having taken his sock off was enjoying scratching away at a sting on his ankle and dreaming of meat pies.

'All right, there's no need to shout,' he grumbled angrily. 'What do you want me to say?'

'I'm not talking to you, you big idiot, I'm talking to the spirits,' she hissed out of the corner of her mouth. Quickly switching back to her dramatic voice, she wailed, 'Hear me, oh mighty ones. Listen to me!'

A couple of curious sheep had gathered at the bottom of the Knoll to watch and listen to this peculiar woman shouting at the top of her lungs, and they decided it was time that they had their say. They *baaaad* very loudly and repeatedly in response, and if Eddie had been around he could've translated their bleats and baas into: 'Could you keep the noise down please? I've got kids here trying to sleep.'

'I can feel the Vibes,' Demonica ranted, ignoring the noisy sheep. 'I can feel the power surging through my veins like electricity as I communicate with this ancient mound of earth to uncover what secrets lie deep inside its belly,' she wailed dramatically.

'Ugh,' was all Dennis could say as he sat watching her. He thought she looked ridiculous.

'Open the portal, I ask of thee,' she wailed again, really getting into it now. 'I bring an offering of a male, a human – well, I think he is – and though he is ugly of face and foul of mouth and of not much use – but I suppose you could get him to scrub floors and stuff, clean the toilets and things – I offer him to you.'

'Hang on,' Dennis said, suddenly realising who Demonica was ranting about. 'Do you mean me, by any chance?'

'Take him,' she howled. 'And show me the portal.'

An evil thought crossed Dennis's mind, and unable to resist the sheer wickedness of it, he slowly stood up. Creeping silently closer to Demonica, he lifted his foot and gave her a shove.

Demonica opened her eyes and let out a loud scream, but as she fell she turned round and grabbed Dennis by the foot, pulling him down with her. Together they bounced down the Knoll over hard clumps of earth and through piles of nettles until they landed in a heap at the bottom, face down in some sheep poo.

'I'm going to kill you,' Demonica spluttered as she wiped sheep poo off her face. 'Look at the state of me. I'm filthy.'

'Well, there's no change there then,' Dennis snapped back. 'You're always filthy, and there was no need to pull me down with you, my shoe and sock are still up there.'

'Pull you down . . .' Demonica was almost screeching now. 'Pull *you* down? What did you expect? You kicked me.'

'It was an accident,' he lied, trying to sound innocent. 'I slipped, and anyway, you were talking a load of gobbledygook up there.' He started to snigger. 'Do you know you've got sheep poo on the end of your nose?' he said, pointing at her and rocking with laughter.

Demonica growled like a dangerous animal. Her normally death-white complexion was turning a deep red, which was a fairly good indication to anyone who knew her that she'd completely lost her cool and was on the attack. Dennis didn't notice these warning signs as he was too busy laughing, and by the time she pounced, it was too late to defend himself.

'Honestly,' one of the sheep said to the other as they watched the pair rolling around on the grass punching, slapping, kicking, biting and pulling each other's hair. 'The way these humans behave, and in front of the little ones as well, they ought to be ashamed of themselves, it's disgusting.'

'And this is the breed who have the nerve to call themselves civilised? You'd never catch a sheep behaving like that,' the other sheep replied. 'Come away, my dears,' she said to the two little lambs peeping at the action from behind the safety of their mothers' legs. 'It's just two silly humans misbehaving yet again.'

CHAPTER TWENTY-FIVE

The journey back to Dungeness took a lot less time than it had taken Demonica and Dennis to get to the Knoll. They'd turned the van round, taken the brakes off, and hoped that freewheeling down the steep hill would kick-start the engine. Now, it's not a straight hill, it's very bendy in places, and as the van gained speed, going faster and faster, they had both screamed their lungs out. Steam had started to seep out of the bonnet and there was a terrible smell of burning rubber coming from the tyres.

'Brake!' Demonica screamed in terror, her knuckles turning white as she gripped the dashboard.

'I *am* braking!' Dennis screamed back. 'But not much seems to be happening.'

Suddenly, and much to their relief, the engine started up just as they reached the bottom. Hauling on the steering wheel as hard as he could, Dennis turned the van to the right, screeching round the corner on two wheels and narrowly avoiding ending up wrapped round a tree in the woods at the bottom of the hill.

The twins were barely speaking to each other when they finally got back home. Dennis had a nasty black eye and quite a lot of cuts and bruises, while Demonica was missing a few clumps of hair and had a split lip.

Dennis sat at the table holding a wet rag to one eye while attempting with his good eye to read the local newspaper he'd found in a bin.

Demonica had taken herself off to the kitchen and, still not convinced that there wasn't any buried treasure to be had, sat down and started to read Old Molly Maggot's *Book of Spells* again. *There must be a way to get the magical portal to open,* she told herself, *there just has to be.* She read the lengthy spell again, only this time she read the small print at the bottom that she'd previously ignored.

'Oh no,' she groaned out loud.

'Don't tell me you're reading that old book again. It's a load of rubbish. There ain't any buried treasure in that Knoll. Having seen it, you must realise that by now.'

Much as she hated to admit it, Demonica had a feeling that

her brother might be right, as to gain safe access to the Knoll and get the treasure, the small print stated that something very particular was needed for the spell to work. Only a certain type of person could go into the Knoll. Joining Dennis at the table, she slammed the book shut and sat down, tapping the tabletop with her fingers as she tried to work out a solution to this problem.

'I wish you'd stop that. It's very annoying.'

'I'm thinking.'

'That must take a lot of effort.'

'Oh, shut your lip,' she said, sighing loudly, too disappointed to even argue with her brother. 'I'm fed up of all my ideas coming to nothing, it's just not fair.'

'Tell your ickle bwuvver what the matter is,' Dennis teased her, grabbing her hand and talking in a baby voice. 'Why she soooo upset?'

'I'll tell you why she's so upset,' she snapped, pulling her hand away. 'Because you're right. I'll never get my hands on that treasure as it requires the most ridiculous sort of person to go in and get it.'

'Who?' Her brother sneered. 'Aladdin and his magic lamp? You've been reading too many fairy tales, you have.'

'Legend has it that a fortune in treasure was buried by

pirates somewhere near Dymchurch,' Demonica explained. 'But a band of smugglers secretly watched them, and as soon as the pirates left, they dug it up and hid it deep in the Knoll.'

'Go on,' Dennis said, yawning as he didn't believe a word of this so-called legend.

'One of the smugglers was also a magician who practised the Dark Arts,' she continued. 'And so, to make doubly sure that the treasure would remain safe, he put a curse on it.'

'Did he now? And what does this curse do?'

'Well, if you must know, this is what the small print says. I'll read it to you as I know you have difficulty understanding big words,' she sniped, opening the book again and reading out loud.

Be a Pirate Queen from across the sea,
For the Knoll to reveal the treasure to thee.
But be you scoundrel, pickpocket or thief,
Then your quest will end in naught but grief.

'Well, apart from the pirate queen bit, you certainly fit the bill,' Dennis said. 'So if I were you, I'd put those talents to good use instead of chasing non-existent treasure. Look here,' he said, holding up the newspaper. 'There's a fête in Ollington

Village and there's a fancy-dress parade with a prize for the best costume. We could dress up and enter the competition, there might be a big cash prize.'

'In Ollington Village?' Demonica raised her eyebrows. 'It's hardly Las Vegas or one of those TV talent shows. I bet first prize is a box of chocolates and a cheap plastic trophy.'

'Probably, but I bet there's lots of handbags and wallets just waiting to be lifted. There might even be a nice juicy collection for a local charity that's just ripe for the picking. So, what do you say, sis? There's no smarter thief than you, so why don't you forget the fairy story and let's get back to real life and to what you're best at, which, as every copper in the country knows, is robbing.'

Demonica sat silently. 'This fancy dress,' she asked eventually. 'What's the theme?'

'Well, funnily enough, it's Pirates and Smugglers,' he replied. 'And there's loads of old stuff upstairs that'll be perfect for it.'

'Great,' she muttered, none-too enthusiastically. 'Do you think if I dressed up as a Pirate Queen, the Knoll would open the portal?' she said, brightening up a little at the idea.

'No chance,' Dennis replied flatly. 'No knoll is that stupid. Now let's go upstairs and find something to wear.'

CHAPTER TWENTY-SIX

There were a few tears from Aunt Budge and Giddy as they said their goodbyes. Giddy said she would come again and Aunt Budge made her promise that she would. Giddy said she would drop in on her way back from France and, if it wasn't inconvenient, could they stay to break up the journey?

'You can sleep in your old room,' Aunt Budge suggested. 'It'll be like old times.'

'As long as I don't have to sleep in a bunk bed,' Giddy said, laughing. 'I'm not built for one of those any more.'

'Goodbye, you two,' Jacob said, shaking Eddie and Flo's hands. 'Enjoy Kent and remember what I said about the Knoll,' he added with a wink. 'Don't go up after dark or the faeries might get you.'

They stood on the steps waving as the red sports car zoomed off down the drive with Giddy honking the horn.

'Thank heavens we haven't any neighbours,' Aunt Budge

said as they watched the car vanish out of sight. 'She makes such an awful racket sounding that horn, but that's Giddy for you. Full of life, with not a care in the world. I wonder what the animals made of her. Let's go in and ask them.'

The fish had been highly impressed with Giddy as she had reminded them of a pirate called Cut-throat Kate, and, in fact, they were sure that she *was* Kate, travelling in disguise under a different name (which, of course, she wasn't).

'It's definitely Kate,' they told anyone who would listen. 'She didn't fool us, and the old man looked a lot like her first mate when they sailed on the good ship *Skuttlefish*. I bet there's a ship waiting in Dover harbour for them right now.'

Butch was in love. Giddy had petted him and carried him and tickled his tummy and fed him little treats, and he would have done anything for her.

Bunty also thought Giddy was marvellous. 'She's an inspiration to all young people,' she exclaimed. 'And her brother is fascinating. Those stories he was telling us – so interesting. Did you know I thought I once saw a fairy?' she said later that morning, casually giving her whiskers a rub as she sat on the arm of the chair. 'I was in the greenhouse with Ralph, one of our officers who was also a keen tomato grower, when something caught my eye.'

'What was it?' Eddie asked.

'What is Bunty saying?' Flo asked. She still got a bit annoyed that she could never join in the conversations.

'She's telling us about something that caught her eye in a greenhouse,' Aunt Budge explained. 'Go on, dear,' she said to Bunty. 'We're all ears.'

'Well, it was hard to tell at first as the sun was so bright,' Bunty explained, delighted that she had an audience. 'But right in the corner, I saw something fluttering about. It was a very elegant creature with large wings and it was trapped in an upturned jam jar, tapping on the glass to get my attention. And what's more, it had a face. Well, you can imagine, I was very excited.'

'So, what happened?' Eddie asked.

'Not a lot,' she replied, slightly embarrassed. 'The fairy turned out to be a very large moth that was trapped in a jam jar. Ralph set it free, and as it flew by me, I could see that it didn't have a face at all. It was simply the creature's markings. Most disappointing.'

'Life can be a disappointment, little hamster,' Louis said, stretched out on the rug. 'And I know, because showbusiness is a ruthless business full of constant disappointments. One minute you're eating glazed carrots and the finest leafy greens and the next thing you know you're munching on hay – not that it's ever happened to me, of course, and nor is it likely to now that I'm a huge star.'

They all groaned out loud – except for Flo, who couldn't understand what Louis had said – as they were so astonished at his complete lack of modesty.

'Twinkle, twinkle little star then,' Butch growled. 'I'm going for a walk.' And he headed outside to dig up something interesting that he'd buried in the garden the day before.

'Well, what are we going to do with the rest of the day?' Flo asked, feeling slightly deflated now the cottage had returned to normal after the whirlwind that was Giddy had driven off. 'Shall we get the bikes out?'

'That's a great idea,' Eddie replied. 'And we can go and have a look at the knoll that Jacob was speaking about.'

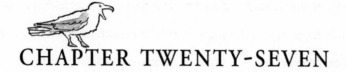

CHAPTER TWENTY-SEVEN

Eddie and Flo set out with Butch sitting proudly in the little basket attached to the front of Eddie's bike. Bunty had decided to join Flo and was sitting on her shoulder holding on to a lock of her hair to steady herself, as they cycled up the steep hill that led to the Knoll.

As there were sheep in the field at the base of the Knoll, Eddie put a lead on Butch, which didn't please the feisty little dog one bit.

'It's the rule,' Eddie explained. 'You must always put your dog on a lead if you're in a field with cattle or sheep.'

'Why?' Butch asked sulkily.

'In case the dog is tempted to chase sheep, not that I'm suggesting you'd do such a thing,' Eddie said. 'But if you did, then the farmer could shoot you.'

'As if I'd chase sheep,' Butch said, scowling. 'And as for the farmer, I'd have them down on the ground before they could even think about reaching for their gun.'

They climbed the Knoll, carefully avoiding the nettles, and reaching the top they stood in silence admiring the panoramic view (unlike the Rancid Twins, who couldn't have cared less).

'It's so beautiful,' Flo murmured as she gazed out across the woods and to the patchwork quilt of fields that made up the Marshes, and on to the Channel beyond.

'You can see why smugglers used to signal from up here to the other smugglers who'd landed at Dymchurch. There wouldn't have been many lights on the Marshes back then, so a flashing lantern would have been easy to see,' Eddie pointed out, fascinated to be standing on something that looked so ordinary, yet had such a long and interesting history.

After a moment, they sat down and tucked into the sandwiches and cakes that Miss Schmidt had insisted they take with them.

'How could you refuse my apple cake?' she'd said, pretending to be upset. 'I've won awards for it, and you might get hungry after such a long journey. I've also packed some fruit and sandwiches and two bottles of juice.'

Eddie tried to explain that they were only going as far as Ollington, and not all the way to Siberia, but Miss Schmidt wouldn't hear of it and now, sitting on top of the Knoll happily eating their sandwiches, they were grateful that she'd gone to the trouble of packing such a delicious picnic.

'What are they?' Flo asked, pointing to an adjoining field.

Eddie looked. 'Oh, they're alpacas,' he said, delighted to see such an unexpected sight in a Kentish field. 'They must belong to the people in that house over there. Let's go and take a closer look,' Eddie suggested, warning Butch not to bark at the alpacas, as if he did then they might spit at him.

They finished their lunch and clambered back down the Knoll. As they walked across the field, Eddie said hello to a few sheep on the way.

'Excuse me,' one of the sheep asked, 'but can you understand me?'

'Perfectly,' Eddie replied.

'Goodness,' the sheep said, more than a little surprised. 'I never thought I'd meet an Intuitive in our field, did you, girls?' she said, turning to the other sheep. 'My name is Doris and these two are my friends, Sandra and Lil.'

'I do hope you're not going to behave as badly as our last visitors,' Sandra said, frowning disapprovingly. (Sheep can frown, have a look the next time you see one.) 'They behaved like hooligans, shouting their heads off on top of the Knoll and fighting.'

'Yes, fighting,' Lil agreed, nodding her head. 'Don't forget the fighting. Really going at each other, they were. They scared the young ones, they did, with their shocking behaviour. We're not used to that in these parts.'

For the thousandth time since she'd known Eddie, Flo asked him what they were all saying and Eddie started to translate.

'I wonder who they were?' Flo asked, and then, desperate to stroke a lamb, she asked the sheep if any of them were theirs.

'Indeed, they are,' Doris replied, even though Flo couldn't understand her. 'Those two over there are mine, Brittany is the one leaping up and down and Adele is the one who's bleating. She always sounds sad, but I can assure you she's not. That one there is little Beryl, she's Sandra's girl, and the one by the fence is Janice.'

'She's my girl,' Lil said proudly. 'Would your friend like to meet them?'

Eddie passed on the message to Flo, who jumped at the chance.

The sheep called out to their lambs and they instantly came running, nutting their mothers' sides in the hope of a quick suck of milk.

Flo slowly held out her hand and very cautiously Janice, the smallest of the lambs, approached her. She sniffed Flo's outstretched hand, wary at first, but as she gained confidence she allowed Flo to gently scratch the top of her head. Janice liked that a lot and in no time at all Flo was cuddling her.

'This is a very special occasion,' Eddie told Flo. 'The sheep don't like the lambs being touched, and it's also against the law to do so unless you're a shepherd or a vet, but today the sheep are allowing it. You're very lucky, Flo.'

'She's so beautiful,' Flo whispered as she gently stroked the little lamb. 'Thank you for allowing me to do this,' she said to Lil. 'I won't forget it, ever.'

Butch had been exceptionally well behaved when meeting the sheep and had sat quietly, keeping his distance a little way from them as he didn't quite trust these woolly monsters.

'Well, it was nice to meet you,' Eddie said to the sheep. 'But we're off to see the alpacas now.'

'Good luck there,' Doris replied. 'They're not very

neighbourly. They can be quite stand-offish. His name is Rufus and her name is . . . wait for it . . . The Princess,' she said, raising her eyes up to the sky.

The alpacas had seen them coming but they preferred to pretend that they hadn't, and instead they kept their heads down, casually nibbling at the grass as if no one was there.

Standing by the fence, Eddie and Flo called out to them, but the alpacas still refused to look up and carried on ignoring them both.

'Don't look, Rufus,' The Princess said under her breath. 'Keep pretending we haven't seen them and they might go away.'

'Come and talk to us,' Eddie pleaded but they still took no notice.

All of a sudden, there was a flash of something black and a flap of wings as a large crow landed on a low-hanging branch.

'Here, you two!' the crow shouted. 'Don't be so snotty and come and say hello to my mates.'

'Stanley!' Butch barked his loudest bark and started to leap, yapping and howling happily.

'Stanley,' Eddie said, delighted to see his old friend. 'You've turned up.'

'Well, I said I would, didn't I?' he croaked back. 'And a crow always keeps his promises. How's tricks?'

CHAPTER TWENTY-EIGHT

Stanley had known exactly where to find Eddie and Flo as he'd flown to the cottage first and Aunt Budge, who could speak Crow, had told him. He'd stopped over in London for a few days to visit his friend the raven in the Tower of London, and then he'd spent a bit of time in Hyde Park with a few pigeons that he was pals with.

'Nice little break it was,' he announced. 'Did me the world of good, and now for a bit of country air. Are you two enjoying yourselves out here in the wild blue yonder? I bet you can't get Deliveroo.'

'We haven't tried,' Eddie replied, laughing. 'And besides, I doubt Miss Schmidt would even allow a takeaway in her kitchen. She'd probably think we didn't like her cooking.'

'Is that boy actually speaking to that crow, or are my eyes deceiving me?' The Princess asked Rufus. She was watching them out of the corner of her eye as she didn't want to be seen staring.

'Well, are you coming over to say hello or what?' Stanley shouted again. 'Or are you still pretending we don't exist? I could come over and land on your back if you'd prefer it.'

'Perish the thought,' Rufus said, shuddering slightly at the very idea. Sighing, he turned to The Princess and said, 'Come, my dear, we'd best go and meet them or we'll get no peace.'

They sashayed slowly towards the fence. They really were a most elegant pair with their long necks and furry coats. The Princess was a rich chocolate brown in colour while Rufus was pure white with a brown patch on his back.

'Good afternoon,' Rufus said, once they'd reached the group. 'My name is Rufus and this is my partner, The Princess.' He bowed his head respectfully when he mentioned her name. 'And might I enquire who you are?'

Eddie didn't say that the sheep had already told them their names, and instead he said, 'It's very nice to meet you. My name's Eddie, Eddie Albert, and this is Flo, she's from Amsterdam. And this is Stanley the crow and these two are Bunty and Butch. We're staying with Lady Buddleia on the Marshes. She's my aunt.' He was gabbling a bit and talking far too fast as he found these two haughty alpacas a little bit intimidating.

'Did you say Lady Buddleia?' Rufus asked.

Eddie nodded.

'Is she a member of the royal family?'

'Well, not exactly,' Eddie tried to explain. 'She married a lord, you see, but she does know the Queen.'

'Interesting,' Rufus drawled, curling his top lip.

'Indeed,' The Princess agreed.

'You don't spit, do you?' Eddie asked. 'It's only that I heard that alpacas spit, and I'd just wondered . . .' His voice trailed off as he realised that he might have put his foot in it.

'Spit!' Rufus exclaimed, highly insulted. 'Spit! We are well-bred alpacas and wouldn't dream of spitting.'

The Princess made a little sound halfway between a sigh and a squeal. 'Oh, dear me,' she moaned. 'Such a word shouldn't be uttered in high society.'

'I'm really, really sorry,' Eddie said quickly. 'It's just that I—'

Flo gave Eddie a nudge in the ribs and interrupted. 'Whatever it is you're talking about, I'd give it up now, if I were you, as going by that alpaca's expression, you're only making things worse.'

If Butch thought the sheep were odd, then these two alpacas looked as if they were from another planet, but Bunty couldn't help admiring their curly mops of curls on the tops of their heads, and wondered to herself if she should grow her fur a bit and attempt the same style herself.

'May I ask what brings you here?' Rufus asked Eddie in a very superior manner, still slightly prickly over the spitting business. 'Apart from the farmer and the odd hillwalker, thankfully we don't see many strangers.'

'We came to have a look at the Knoll,' Eddie replied. 'We've heard so many stories about it, so we thought we'd pay it a visit.'

'What is the interest in the Knoll all of a sudden?' The Princess said. 'There were two humans here not so long ago, adult humans, not that we paid them any attention of course, they were far too vulgar for our liking.'

'Yes, the sheep said something about that,' Eddie said. 'They told me that the pair of them were fighting. The sheep said they had a row with them.'

'I'm not in the least bit surprised that the sheep would get involved in an argument,' The Princess replied with a snort. 'They'd enjoy that sort of thing, squabbling in public. I'm afraid the sheep are quite common and not the sort we mix with,' she added, lifting her head proudly.

Eddie thought that she looked like a very grand duchess – all she needed was a tiara and a fan. While they might be a pair of outrageous snobs, they were certainly extraordinary animals.

'Well, it's been nice talking to you, but we'd best be off now.' Eddie said, looking at his watch. 'My aunt will be wondering where we've got to.'

'Do pass on our very best wishes to her ladyship,' Rufus

said, bowing his head. 'And if she's ever passing this way then please ask her to call on us.'

'Righty-ho,' said Eddie. 'I'll tell her, as I'm sure she'd love to meet you. Bye!'

And with that, they set off for home.

'The sun will be setting soon,' Stanley remarked, hopping on to the handlebars of Eddie's bicycle. 'Best get out of here, as we wouldn't want the fairies to get us, would we? I've heard it's not safe after dark. Your Aunty Budge was telling me all about the stories that old man was filling your heads with,' he added with a wink and a cackle. Then, launching himself off the handlebars, he flew high above the trees. 'See you back at the cottage,' he cawed before vanishing into the woods.

CHAPTER TWENTY-NINE

I t was the morning of the Ollington Village Fête. A great wicker basket had arrived from the theatrical costumes company in London the day before, full of an assortment of costumes.

Eddie and Flo had rummaged through the basket, trying on lots of different outfits until finally Eddie had settled on a striped top with black trousers and a pair of swashbuckler's boots. He'd found a spotted scarf which he wrapped round his head and tied in a knot at the back, just like a real pirate. Strapped to his belt was a convincing cutlass made of plastic. He'd also found a black moustache, which he'd stuck on with the special glue that it came with, but it had tickled his nose and kept slipping whenever Eddie spoke, before eventually falling off all together and ending up stuck to Butch's tail, who had a busy time chasing it until Flo removed it for him.

Flo looked spectacular. She'd picked a long, flowing black

skirt with purple and red petticoats underneath, a baggy white blouse and a large leather belt slung round her hips with a holster containing a fake flintlock pistol. She also wore an eye patch and a large black pirate's hat with a purple feather in. She looked quite fearsome, and the fish were completely won over by this new Flo.

'You could be the daughter of Anne Bonny,' Dan said, wide-eyed with awe.

'Who's Anne Bonny?' Eddie asked. 'Was she a pirate?'

'One of the worst,' Jake said with relish as he joined his brother hanging over the top of the tank. 'She sailed with Calico Jack Rackham. Notorious she was round the waters of Old Jamaica.'

Eddie repeated this to Flo, who bared her teeth and growled at them. 'Ya wanna walk the plank, me hearties?' she snarled in a lousy attempt at a pirate accent and then laughed as the fish plopped quickly back into the water.

Butch was proudly wearing a black bandana round his neck that had a skull and crossbones on, while Bunty, having been inspired by Flo, was wearing her large-brimmed hat that had once sat on a doll's head, with a feather of Stanley's that he had given her, trimmed down to size and stuck in the side.

'Well, I think we all look splendid,' Aunt Budge announced, sweeping into the room. 'Perfectly splendid, we shall do the village proud riding on the float through the streets.' They all looked at Aunt Budge in amazement. She was wearing a long dress with lots of frills and ruffles, and she was carrying a matching parasol. But what really grabbed their attention was her white, powdered wig with a little ringlet that hung over her shoulder and the jaunty little hat that was balanced on top.

'Do I look all right?' she asked coyly. 'It's not too much is it?'

They all agreed she looked sensational.

'But what are you supposed to be?' Eddie asked, as she didn't look much like a pirate to him.

'Well, dear, pirates always frequented a favoured dockside inn, a safe place for them to plan their next move or stash away their stolen loot, so I'm dressed as the innkeeper – the one who keeps an eye on the door in case any customs men should wander in as I serve villainous rapscallions tankards of ale.'

'You mean like bar staff?' Eddie asked, still slightly puzzled.

'No, dear,' Aunt Budge replied. 'More on the managerial side. Now, are we ready, as Whetstone has brought the car round. They do like you to arrive in style at these things, and Miss Schmidt is waiting for us outside. And as the fish are in their travelling tank, I think we're ready for the off.'

'Wait a minute,' Louis said from the sofa. 'I've decided to come.' He hadn't wanted to go at first, but when he'd heard Aunt Budge mention riding on a float, he'd changed his mind. Why, this was a chance for the public to adore him and there were bound to be photo opportunities with the press, so he'd convinced himself that he owed it to his fans to make an appearance.

'I'll carry him,' Flo offered. 'He'd look good as a pirate's pet.'

Miss Schmidt was a sight to behold. She was wearing her usual cook's apron, only she'd drawn a skull and crossbones on the front with a Sharpie. Round her head, she'd wound a black scarf and had a gold earring dangling from her right ear. She certainly looked the part and would probably scare any pirate – should she ever come across one – half to death.

'I'm the ship's cook,' she told them, with a blank expression on her face. 'And Whetstone, in case you're wondering, is the ship's doctor,' she added, pointing at Whetstone who was wearing a black top hat and a dusty-looking tailcoat.

'I don't like top hats,' Louis groaned. 'And neither would you if you'd been crushed inside one and then yanked out by your ears twice daily.'

'Indeed,' Bunty replied. 'I can't imagine it.'

'Well, I'm sure you'll all do splendidly,' Aunt Budge replied, a little uncertain. 'Now, let's get going, I have to open the fête at midday, and I hate to be late.'

CHAPTER THIRTY

There was a great turnout for the fête with lots of people dressed as smugglers and pirates. The float turned out to be the back of a lorry decked out to resemble a ship, with a large throne in the middle for whichever lucky person won the competition and was crowned the King or Queen of the Pirates.

'Hey, they have a band,' Flo said when she saw a small stage lined with musical instruments. 'Great! We can dance.'

Eddie gave her a weak smile. He wasn't keen on dancing, except when he was alone, and he reminded himself to hide if any dancing started up.

They had a walk around the stalls: they were selling a wide variety of things, from home-made cakes and jams, or candles and soaps to patchwork quilts that the women of the village had made themselves.

Miss Schmidt was very interested in the cake and jam stall.

She was given a slice of lemon drizzle to sample and she stood with eyes closed, slowly chewing a small piece. She took her time, savouring the flavour with an expert's palate, which made the woman on the stall a bit nervous.

'*Wunderbar*,' Miss Schmidt said at last.

'Eh?' the woman replied.

'Your cake,' Miss Schmidt told her, 'is the work of a true artiste. I'll take two lemon drizzles and half a dozen scones, please.'

To Eddie and Flo's delight the alpacas were there with the couple who owned them.

'We're being shown off, and you can have something called a selfie with me for a pound, with all the money going to charity.' Rufus yawned as he explained to Eddie. He seemed bored and obviously considered the whole affair extremely undignified.

'I feel cheap,' The Princess moaned. 'Posing for photos with complete strangers. I'm tempted to "you know what" at them.'

'No, what?' Rufus asked.

'You know,' she said, lowering her voice. 'The "S" word.'

'Swear?' Eddie offered.

'No,' she answered, almost shouting now with frustration. 'Spit!'

'Oh, my dear,' Rufus admonished. 'Control yourself; remember who you are.'

However, both of them perked up when Eddie introduced them to Aunt Budge. 'How charming,' she said graciously in her poshest voice. 'And what a privilege to meet such dignified, elegant alpacas as yourselves.'

Aunt Budge couldn't understand Alpaca. She understood Camel, but when it came to Alpaca she didn't have a clue, so to play it safe she kept saying, 'How utterly charming,' and 'What a treat, delighted I'm sure.'

Of course, the alpacas lapped this up, and from then on they referred to Aunt Budge as, 'Our dear friend, Lady Buddleia.'

Aunt Budge was beginning to flap as it had gone half past twelve and she was supposed to have officially opened the fête at noon. Pushing through the crowd towards her came an extremely flustered event organiser, who looked like he was in a bit of a panic.

'It's the band,' he explained. 'They were here earlier to do a soundcheck and set up their instruments, but they went off to have a spot of lunch somewhere, and anyway, they've been in a crash. Thankfully, none of them are seriously hurt, but they've been taken to the William Harvey Hospital anyway, which means we have no band. What am I going to do?' he wailed.

'Calm down while I think of a solution,' Aunt Budge advised. 'Wipe the sweat off your forehead, straighten your tie, get up on that stage and announce me.'

The event organiser did as he was told. He had a bit of trouble with the sound at first as the microphone screeched and wailed like the siren in the ghost train.

'He needs to move away from the speakers,' Aunt Budge remarked. 'That's why he's getting so much feedback, plus he's holding that mic too close to his mouth.'

'How do you know about technical things like this,' Eddie asked, surprised.

'Oh, when I was a young girl, for a brief period in my life and to help pay my way through university, I would appear in little summer shows. I was even in a pantomime once, although I have to admit, I wasn't very good, which probably explains why I was cast as the back end of Clara the Cow.'

'You were on the stage, and you went to university.' Eddie was astonished, as he didn't know any of this.

'Yes, dear,' she replied. 'I got a BA (Hons) in Archaeology, that's how I met my husband. I was assigned to help him on a dig in Egypt, and as for the stage, well, put it this way, Dame Maggie Smith didn't feel threatened. Now hush, dear, I'm on in a minute.'

There was a lot of mumbling when it was announced that the band wouldn't be appearing, but Aunt Budge got a nice round of applause when she was introduced to the stage. She made the usual, 'I now declare this fête open' speech, and then started chatting to the crowd. She was really very good, and even managed to tell a few jokes and raise a laugh.

'I know you're all terribly disappointed that the band aren't here,' Eddie heard her saying, 'but their instruments are, and it seems a terrible shame to waste them, so this is what I propose . . .' And to Eddie's horror he heard her call out his name along with Flo's, Whetstone's and Miss Schmidt's, telling them all to come up on stage and join her.

CHAPTER THIRTY-ONE

E ddie looked at Flo with panic in his eyes. 'I'm not getting up there,' he cried. 'I'll die of shame.'

'You'll die of boredom if you don't take a chance when an unexpected opportunity comes along,' a voice boomed from behind him. It was Miss Schmidt. 'Now, come along. You too, Flo, your aunt needs you both.' And grabbing them each by the hand, she dragged them on stage.

Eddie stood frozen to the spot with a strange grin on his face as Aunt Budge introduced them. He glanced at Flo, who didn't seem to be the least bit bothered, quite the opposite in fact, as she seemed to be enjoying herself. Aunt Budge even introduced all the animals, who got a huge cheer from the crowd.

Bunty, who was sitting on Eddie's head, gave them all a little wave, but Louis, who had been lying on top of the piano, stood up on his hind paws, blew the crowd a kiss and then bowed deeply. 'Thank you for coming to see me,' he said, believing that the applause was strictly for him alone. 'But, please, no touching.'

The fish were zipping around their travel tank like miniature jet skis, as they were so happy to be among so many pirates, and Stanley, who had just flown in, was practising a few dance steps with Butch.

'Now,' Aunt Budge was saying. 'My nephew, Eddie, is a marvel on guitar.'

'No, I'm not,' Eddie protested, having found his voice.

'Don't argue, dear,' Aunt Budge said. 'And his friend Flo here is a wonder on the trumpet.'

Flo just stood open-mouthed.

'And Miss Schmidt would put Ringo Starr to shame on the drums, wouldn't you, dear?'

Miss Schmidt cracked her knuckles and nodded in agreement.

'And last but not least is Whetstone, who plays the piano with the skill of a concert pianist. So then, what would you say to a little song?'

The crowd cheered enthusiastically.

'What are we playing?' an extremely anxious Eddie whispered to Aunt Budge.

'Oh, don't worry,' she replied casually. 'Just follow me.'

Just follow me? Eddie was panic-stricken at the sea of expectant faces, all of them staring back at him waiting for him to play something.

In that moment, he didn't know what to do. Should he make a run for it? Or maybe he could pretend to faint? Suddenly, he remembered what his dad had said, *Why don't you show them what you're made of? Give them a bit of the old rock-and-roll? You're good, Eddie, very good.*

With his dad's advice ringing in his ears, Eddie slowly picked up the electric guitar from its stand. It was heavier than his own guitar, but it felt good to hold and he played a few chords to see if it needed tuning.

It sounded magnificent, and somebody in the crowd let out a loud howl of approval. He played a few more chords as he tuned it and, happy that it sounded right, he let rip and went wild.

Flo looked at him in disbelief, as did Miss Schmidt, who dropped one of her drumsticks. The crowd whistled and cheered, and with his new-found confidence, Eddie felt like a rock star.

'Well done, Eddie!' Aunt Budge said. 'Now, are we ready? Then let's go. Mr Whetstone, if you please.'

Whetstone played a little introduction for her, and Aunt Budge began to sing, quite softly at first.

I danced twice nightly in a show,
In a chorus line on the pier, you know.
But I gave up the theatre when I got myself wed,
And dug up mummies in Egypt instead.
You might possibly think now I'm old and grey,
That this old fossil has had her day.
But believe you me, as you're about to discover,
You certainly shouldn't judge a book by its cover.

Then taking a deep breath she shouted, 'Hit it!'

On cue, Miss Schmidt went wild on the drums. Flo joined in on her trumpet, and it wasn't long before Eddie had picked the tune up and was giving his all on the guitar. Stanley was croaking loudly, although he liked to call it singing, and Butch was howling away like a little wolf. The crowd roared.

'Don't judge a book by its cover,' Aunt Budge sang.

Don't judge a lady when she hits a certain age,
Cos although I look sedate,

I'm not past my sell-by date.

I can still do the can-can, you don't believe me?

Just watch me, mate.

Here she paused, telling Eddie and Flo to stop for a moment and, signalling to Whetstone to play a lively can-can tune, she hoisted her skirts and kicked her legs up high.

Eddie and Flo couldn't believe it. Neither could the

audience, who went bananas. But it was nothing compared to the reaction Aunt Budge got when she finished her dance with a perfect cartwheel that ended in the splits.

'Okay,' she shouted to 'the band', as she jumped up from the floor. 'Give it all you've got, kids.'

'They couldn't take it,' Miss Schmidt yelled.

'One, two, three, four,' Aunt Budge shouted and started to sing again.

It's so lovely here in Kent,
It's a place that's heaven-sent.
But don't think that I'll be sitting,
Watching telly as I'm knitting.
There's a big world to discover,
So, listen to me, brother,
Don't judge a book,
Turn the pages, take a look,
Just don't judge a book by its cover.

The crowd could be heard cheering and whistling for miles.

'Oh dear,' sniffed Rufus disapprovingly, watching from his pen. 'How disappointing. She's a theatrical.'

CHAPTER THIRTY-TWO

Another couple in the crowd weren't too impressed with Aunt Budge, either. It was the Rancid Twins, Dennis and Demonica, dressed in a strange array of old clothes that they'd found in Molly Maggot's wardrobe. People weren't standing too close to the pair as the musty fumes coming off them were overpowering.

'Silly old bag,' Dennis growled, watching Aunt Budge taking her bows. 'Do you remember her and her hard-faced kids when we broke down on the road, and she wouldn't help me push the van.'

'Yes, selfish, you see? Just because she's loaded she thinks she can treat people like muck. That rabbit looks tasty though,' Demonica replied, eyeing Louis up. 'It'd make a lovely stew with a few carrots.'

Just then, the event organiser announced that the parade was about to start.

'Let's lift a few wallets and purses while the crowd are watching the parade,' Dennis suggested. 'They won't even notice as they'll be too interested in what's going on.'

'Suckers,' Demonica cackled. 'Yeah, let's fleece them of their hard-earned cash.'

There weren't that many floats, but they were certainly lively. The school had one, as did the local pub, and there were a few tractors and people in open-topped cars waving. But the biggest float was the lorry that Eddie and the gang were on. Before the floats started to move, the event organiser got on the lorry with a megaphone.

'It's time to reveal the winner of the best-dressed pirate or smuggler,' he announced. 'After a lot of thought, the judges, who have been wandering among you, have come to the unanimous decision—'

'Get on with it,' someone shouted from the crowd.

'. . . that this year's winner, to be crowned Queen of the Pirates is . . .' He paused for effect. 'The young lady from Holland . . . Flo!'

Flo couldn't believe it. She was part embarrassed and part stunned by the judges' decision.

'Well done, Flo!' Eddie cheered, and Aunt Budge hugged her.

'Right, while they're all busy cheering, get in there now – there's a handbag in front of you that's just waiting to be picked,' Dennis hissed to his sister, but Demonica wasn't listening to him. She was busy concentrating on Flo, who was being lifted on to the throne and having a crown placed on her head by somebody dressed as a mermaid.

'All hail the Pirate Queen,' a man shouted. 'All hail Dutch Flo, Queen of the Pirates.'

A voice in Demonica's head was quoting from the spell book, *A Pirate Queen from Across the Sea*, over and over again. *That's it*, she thought, a light shining in her dark beady eyes. *She's the one, she's the Pirate Queen from across the sea.*

'What are you waiting for?' Dennis demanded angrily. 'Get that bag before the woman moves on. What's the matter with you? Lost your nerve?'

'Never mind bags,' Demonica replied. 'Bring the van round. I want that girl.'

CHAPTER THIRTY-THREE

'Congratulations!' Demonica gushed as soon as she got Flo on her own. Flo had posed for photographs for the local press and had also had quite a few selfies with admirers, and for the brief moment that Flo wasn't surrounded by people, Demonica seized her chance.

'My name is Monica Chatterbox,' Demonica said, taking Flo by the arm and gently leading her away. 'I work for a wonderful magazine called *Abandoned Furry Friends*, and my readers would just love a photo with you and your gorgeous rabbit. My photographer is just getting his equipment ready in the van,' she said, directing Flo towards the van.

This woman is certainly pushy, Flo thought, and even though she was slightly suspicious of this 'Monica Chatterbox' – who smelled very strange and looked even stranger – for once, she didn't trust her instincts. Instead, even though she knew she shouldn't go off with a stranger, she allowed herself to be led away and, more or less bullied into having a photo taken. Flo thought that the van looked familiar, but then didn't all black vans look the same?

'Are you ready to take our young friend's photo?' Demonica called to a man who was bent over and seemed to be looking for something inside the back of the van.

'Just sorting his camera out,' Demonica told Flo in a cheery voice, shoving her towards the van. 'Won't take a minute.'

Just as Flo reached the back of the van, the man turned round. He was wearing a mask over his eyes, the kind highwaymen wear, but even so, Flo recognised him immediately.

'Hey,' she said accusingly. 'You're that man who was rude to Aunt Budge in Dungeness.'

But before she could say any more or turn and run, he'd pulled a sack over her head and bundled her into the back of the van. Demonica jumped in after her, pulling the doors closed.

'Put your foot down,' she ordered Dennis as he turned the ignition on and started the van. 'It's rabbit stew for dinner, and a chest full of smugglers' gold for us tonight.'

*

After a short while, Eddie noticed that Flo was missing, and going in search of her he bumped into the alpacas again.

'You haven't seen Flo, the girl I was with, have you?' he asked Rufus.

'I have, now you mention it,' he replied casually. 'She was being kidnapped. Along with a big fluffy rabbit.'

'Kidnapped!' Eddie shouted in disbelief. 'What do you mean?'

'I mean what I say,' Rufus replied. 'Thanks to my beautiful long neck I can see over the hedge and on to the road. There were two humans, and one of them put your friend and the rabbit in a sack and then they drove off with her in a van.'

Eddie couldn't believe what he was hearing.

'I think they were those ghastly humans who were on the Knoll the other day,' The Princess said. 'The ones who were fighting and swearing. I thought they might be just playing a game with your friend, but going by your concern, apparently they weren't.'

Eddie rushed off to find Aunt Budge to tell her what the alpacas had said. Together they searched the grounds to be sure Flo wasn't there and kept trying to ring her on her mobile, but there was no answer (which wasn't surprising as Demonica had thrown it out of the van).

Whetstone and Miss Schmidt drove around in the car, but there was no sign of Flo, she'd simply vanished. Aunt Budge was really beginning to worry so she approached a nearby policeman to report Flo's disappearance.

'You say she's dressed as a pirate and carrying a large rabbit?' he said, scratching his head. 'And you reckon she's been kidnapped by two people in a large van? Did you witness this, young man?' he asked Eddie.

Eddie blushed, he wasn't much good when it came to telling a lie, but he couldn't admit that an alpaca had told him, could he? The policeman would've thought Eddie was wasting his time.

'Er, yes,' he stammered. 'A black van, just over there.'

'Did you get the registration?'

'Erm, no, I didn't, I'm afraid,' Eddie said, blushing an even deeper red.

'I'll put a search out for her,' the policeman said, not quite believing Eddie. 'But I think you'll find she'll be waiting for you at home. If she doesn't turn up, then give us a call immediately. Good afternoon, madam,' he said to Aunt Budge, giving her a little salute and walking away.

They all headed back to the cottage to see if Flo was there, but just as they suspected, she wasn't.

'How am I going to explain her disappearance to her parents?' Aunt Budge moaned, pacing up and down the room. 'I'll give her a few more hours and if she doesn't show up, then I'm ringing the police.'

'But she won't show up,' Eddie protested. 'She's been kidnapped, the alpacas said so.'

'Then we must search for clues,' Aunt Budge said, sitting

down and going over things in her mind. 'A black van, you say? Didn't we encounter a repulsive little man in Dungeness with a broken-down black van?'

'Yes, we did,' Eddie agreed. 'And there was a woman in the van with him too. We heard her shouting.'

'Anything else we know about them?' Aunt Budge asked. 'The more details we have, the better.'

'Well, the alpacas said that they were the same couple who were up on the Knoll fighting.'

'Why were they up there?' Aunt Budge wondered, rubbing her chin thoughtfully. 'Obviously up to no good.'

'Stanley can help us, can't you, Stan?' Eddie said to the crow who was perched on the back of the armchair listening intently to what was going on. 'You've done it before.'

'Say no more,' Stanley replied. 'I know exactly what you want me to do. You want me to have a look around Dungeness to see if I can spot anything suspicious.'

'Right on, Stanley,' Aunt Budge said. 'You really are a marvel.'

'All in a day's work,' he cawed, and flying out of the window he headed off for Dungeness.

Eddie felt hopeless. He couldn't just sit there and wait, he had to do something, and so he asked Aunt Budge if it was okay to take his bike out and go looking for Flo.

'That's fine,' Aunt Budge said. 'But don't do anything rash, and don't be out for too long, I'd like you back before dark, please.'

CHAPTER THIRTY-FOUR

Demonica and Dennis didn't find it as easy as they'd thought getting Flo out of the van. Even though they'd tied her in a sack, she wriggled and kicked out until eventually she'd managed to get her legs free.

'Grab her,' Demonica ordered as her brother tried to hold Flo down. 'Don't tell me you can't handle a kid.'

Flo might have been scared and confused, but she certainly wasn't going to let these two know it, nor was she giving in without a fight. But between the two of them, and after a lot of struggling, they eventually managed to get both Flo and Louis into the house and into the little room that led off from the kitchen.

'She's a feisty one, I'll give her that,' Dennis said, rubbing his chin where Flo had punched him. 'And that rabbit's got a nasty kick on him too.'

'Well, she won't be causing us any more trouble now that

we've got her all nicely tied up,' Demonica cackled.

Flo sat, tied up on the floor. Louis had been dumped in an empty barrel, which was quite deep so he couldn't escape. 'I must be the unluckiest rabbit in the world,' he moaned. 'I keep getting put into a sack, or a pillowcase and thrown in the back of a vehicle. How many times can a rabbit be kidnapped?'

'Why have you kidnapped us,' Flo demanded, kicking her legs to try and loosen the rope. 'Is it for money? Are you going to hold us to ransom?'

'Well, you see, it's like this,' Demonica said, crouching down to get closer. 'I suppose you could say that this is about money, a fortune in buried treasure, to be exact.'

'And what's that got to do with me?'

'Because you, my little Pirate Queen, are going to get it for me.'

'No, I'm not,' a defiant Flo snapped back.

'Oh, but you will,' Demonica threatened. 'Let me explain why I need you.' And she began to tell Flo all about the spell book and the key to unlocking the buried treasure in the Knoll.

Flo sat staring at Demonica blankly. Was this woman for real? Did she honestly believe all this treasure stuff?

'And as the treasure is cursed and only a Pirate Queen from across the sea can claim it, you're the obvious candidate for the job. You understand?'

'I understand that you're weird,' Flo replied. 'Seriously weird.'

Dennis started to giggle. 'You can say that again. She's weird all right.'

'Shut up,' Demonica snarled. 'I'd sooner be weird than uglier than a toad eating a slug.'

'There's no need for that,' Dennis replied in a huff. 'If I'm ugly then you must be ugly. We are twins, after all.'

Demonica ignored him and turning back to Flo she said, 'You won't be here for long. As soon as it gets dark, we're going for a little ride up to Ollington Knoll where you are going to fetch the treasure.'

'You're wasting your time. I'm not a real Pirate Queen,' Flo reminded her. 'I'm only pretending.'

'That doesn't matter in the least,' Demonica said, her knees cracking as she stood up straight. 'You've been proclaimed the Pirate Queen, and that's good enough for me. Now, keep quiet, or I'll be forced to gag you with a pair of Dennis's old underpants.'

'I doubt that,' Dennis said.

'Why?'

'Because I've only got one pair and I'm wearing them.'

'Fool,' Demonica hissed. 'We're going to leave you now,' she said to Flo, smiling slyly and locking the door behind her as they left. 'But we'll be back for you soon, and stay quiet.'

Flo wriggled around a bit to try and get comfortable, wondering what to do next. Looking around, she guessed that this room had once been a pantry where food was stored. It was filthy now and full of rubble, and there were bars up against the broken window.

The barrel that Louis had been dumped in stank of vinegar.

'Is it my destiny in life,' he moaned dramatically, 'to die in a barrel that reeks of vinegar? How the mighty are fallen.'

Of course, Flo couldn't understand him, and instead she sat watching the skies grow darker through the open window with a worried expression on her face.

'Be strong,' she told herself. 'There's a way out of this somehow, there has to be.'

CHAPTER THIRTY-FIVE

Stanley had covered most of the Marshes in search of a black van and was now circling over Dungeness, but so far he'd been unlucky. Flying around the lighthouse, he headed towards the power station, landing on the top so he could survey the area.

'Where could they be?' he wondered to himself. 'I'd best fly down and ask the locals if they know anything.'

There was a seagull sitting on a table outside the pub.

'Excuse me, mate,' Stanley asked, landing beside him. 'You haven't seen a girl in a pirate costume, have you? Two people nabbed her at the Ollington Fête and drove off with her in a black van.'

'I can't say that I have,' the seagull replied. He was preoccupied keeping his eyes on the door of the pub, waiting for someone to come out with fish and chips. 'Maybe it was

the police in that black van nicking her for being a pirate. It is illegal, you know.'

'No, she's not a real pirate, she was in fancy dress,' Stanley told him. 'And it wasn't the police.'

'Oh,' the seagull said absently, growing bored of waiting for an unsuspecting person to pass with a nice bag of chips for him to swoop on.

'Well, maybe you've seen something unusual, y'know something out of the ordinary,' Stanley pressed on, hoping to get some information out of this annoying bird.

'Well, it depends what you mean by out of the ordinary.'

'Like anybody strange, or new people to the area?' Stanley was growing more frustrated by the second.

'Sorry, nobody springs to mind, apart from that odd couple of humans who live in that old house behind the power station.'

Stanley was exasperated, but thanking the seagull he took off for the power station and after flying around it once, he suddenly spotted a crumbling old house with a battered black van parked outside. 'Gotcha!'

Peeping cautiously into one of the broken windows, he watched and listened to the people inside. It was the Rancid Twins, arguing as usual.

'What are we going to do with the kid once we've got the treasure, that's if it exists,' Dennis was saying.

'I've got plans for her,' Demonica said.

'What are you going to do with your share of the loot?' Dennis asked, rubbing his hands together greedily. 'Where are you going? I can't decide between the south of France, or Rio, or even Argentina, but I'd better make my mind up as I'm going to be away for a long time, so it'd better be somewhere that I'll like.'

Oh, you're going away for a long time, that's for sure, Demonica thought to herself. *But it won't be somewhere nice, it'll be straight back into prison.*

Demonica had made plans. Once she had the treasure, they'd return to the house with Flo, and having made a little sleeping potion out of various herbs she'd found in the overgrown garden following a recipe in the spell book, she intended to drug her brother and leave him tied up with Flo. Then she would catch the first boat out of Dover, but not before she'd sold whatever was in that treasure chest to a man she knew who dealt in stolen jewellery. She was convinced that this treasure would be worth a fortune, and once she was safely out of the way, somewhere in Switzerland, she'd make an anonymous phone call to the police telling them where to find Flo and putting all the blame for kidnapping her on Dennis.

'It's nearly time,' Demonica announced. 'Get the van out and we'll get the girl.'

'I've had a good idea,' Dennis said brightly. 'Why don't we use the rabbit as an offering to make whatever's in that Knoll happy?' Dennis was growing a little nervous now as he wasn't sure what to expect. What if his sister was right? What if there was a magical portal that opened up to reveal buried treasure? Maybe there was some truth in that old spell book?

He'd soon find out, he told himself.

Stanley flew quickly around each window until he came to the pantry with Flo and Louis inside. Landing on the windowsill, he stuck his beak between the bars and croaked loudly.

'Stanley,' a delighted Flo exclaimed. 'Can you help us?'

Stanley nodded and cawed.

'I can't understand you like Eddie, but can you fly and get help? Hurry, as they're taking me to Ollington Knoll to find some stupid treasure.'

'And please be quick,' Louis moaned from inside the barrel. 'I'm beginning to stink of vinegar, and it's ruining my lovely fur.'

As Stanley took to the skies once more, the door opened

and Demonica and Dennis walked in.

'Are you ready, little one?' Demonica asked Flo in a sickly-sweet voice. 'Ready to take the journey of a lifetime into the unknown and claim the treasure for your poor Aunty Demonica?'

'And don't forget poor Uncle Dennis,' her brother reminded her, poking Demonica in the back. 'Split fifty-fifty, remember.'

'I haven't forgotten,' she replied slyly. 'Now grab the brat and the rabbit, there's work to be done.'

CHAPTER THIRTY-SIX

tanley flew as fast as he could. A wind was building up, but as it was a tailwind it helped speed him along. Heading towards Aunt Budge's house, he noticed a light from a bicycle going along the marsh road.

I bet that's Eddie, he thought, and flew down to take a better look.

It *was* Eddie, and he spotted Stanley flying down towards him and stopped cycling.

'Any luck?' he asked the bird anxiously. 'Any sign of Flo and Louis?'

'I've found them,' he replied, landing on Eddie's handlebars. 'These two creeps are taking them to Ollington Knoll . . . something to do with buried treasure.'

'Then I'd better get up there,' Eddie said, getting back on his bike, 'and save them.'

'Hang on a minute,' Bunty said. She'd been sitting on his

shoulder, hanging on to the strap of his cycle helmet as they sped along the lanes. Eddie's electric bike could go quite fast. 'Don't you think you're being a bit hasty? Shouldn't we call for reinforcements before we confront these villains?'

'We don't need re-in whatever you called them,' Butch growled from the little basket on the front of the bike. 'We can easily deal with these bandits ourselves. Let me at them. I'll run them out of town.'

Stanley agreed with Bunty, but before he could say anything, Eddie had sped off on his bike leaving him flapping in the wind.

'Oh well,' he sighed. 'There's only one thing for it. I'd better get after them and save the day, as usual.'

The Rancid Twins had already arrived at the Knoll with Flo and Louis. Demonica had walked right round the hill trying to determine where the best spot for a magical portal could be. Shining her torch, she came across what looked like a large crease carved in the side of the Knoll and had reached the conclusion that she'd discovered the right place.

'Bring the girl and the rabbit over here,' she ordered Dennis as she flicked through the pages of the spell book to find the required incantation. 'And make sure they don't escape.'

Dennis dragged Flo and Louis over to the spot where Demonica wanted them.

'Now, be a good little girl and do as I say, and you won't get hurt. Understand?' she warned Flo, who glared back at her and said something rude, but very appropriate, in Dutch.

Doris, Lil and Sandra, who were, if you remember, the friendly sheep, gathered in a group nearby, curious to see what was going on.

'That's those two awful humans who were here the other day,' Doris said, eyeing them suspiciously. 'What are they doing back here in the dark?'

'And why is that young girl with them?' Sandra asked. 'They don't seem like suitable friends for such a nice little human to me.'

'I think she's in trouble,' Lil guessed correctly. 'Let's go over, ladies, and find out what they're up to.'

'Will you keep still?' Demonica said to Flo as she struggled. 'I'm warning you, if you don't do as I say then that rabbit of yours is going to get it.'

'Demonica,' Dennis said nervously, tapping his sister on

the shoulder. 'There's a load of sheep staring at us, and they don't look very happy.'

'Don't tell me you're scared of sheep?' Demonica scoffed. 'What harm can a sheep do?'

Quite a lot in fact, as they were about to find out.

'Okay,' Lil said, a grim expression on her face. 'Let's give these humans a little nudge. You know what to do, adopt the position, heads down, girls, and CHARGE!!!'

Before Demonica knew it, Lil had butted her hard in the backside, sending her flying across the grass. Sandra and Doris

were chasing Dennis, who took off screaming down the field.

'Help!' he wailed. 'Mad sheep!'

Flo seized her chance to escape, and grabbing Louis, she ran like the wind in the direction of the gate.

Demonica, having picked herself up off the floor, grabbed a branch that was lying nearby.

'Get back,' she hissed at Lil, waving the heavy branch around. 'Or I may be tempted to take a few of those little lambs home with me. They'd be nice served up roasted with a dollop of mint sauce and some peas.'

Lil flared her nostrils and snorted. She was going to butt this horrible human so hard she'd end up in the next field.

'My brother's out there, running wild in the field,' Demonica continued, goading Lil. 'And he hates lambs. It would be awful if he hurt one.'

Lil's immediate instinct was to protect her lamb and although she really wanted to butt this human, she had no choice but to return to her lamb and keep her safe. Giving Demonica one final angry snort, she turned and ran off to warn the others.

'Odd that,' Demonica said out loud to herself. 'It was almost as if that stupid animal understood me. Now, where's that girl gone? And where is my stupid brother?'

'Your stupid brother is right here,' Dennis said, coming round the Knoll. 'And look what he's caught.' He was holding Flo by the hair in one hand and Louis by the ears in the other.

'Be careful with my ears, you ignorant fool,' Louis was shouting. 'They're insured for thousands.'

'Those sheep gave up in the end, and I nabbed this one just as she was heading for the gate,' he said, panting and out of breath. 'She's a nightmare, punched me right in the stomach she did.'

Demonica had completely run out of what little patience she had left. She was angry now, very angry, and two burning spots of rage had appeared on her cheeks.

'On your knees, punk,' she snapped, dragging Flo down, her dark beady eyes blazing. 'It's time for you to get me my treasure.'

Dennis coughed. 'Our treasure you mean,' he reminded his sister. 'And I think I'll go to Rio with my share, what do you think?'

Demonica thought that she was about to explode with rage, but instead she closed her eyes and took a few deep breaths.

When she was calm, she opened her eyes and said, 'Hold her tight and prepare yourself. The moon is full and the time is right, and I'm about to perform Ancient Magic!'

CHAPTER THIRTY-SEVEN

'What was it your dad said, Eddie?' Bunty asked. 'Something about keeping out of trouble, wasn't it? And now here we are heading straight towards it.'

'Bring it on,' Butch yapped, standing up in the basket with the wind making his ears flap. 'Go faster, Eddie. Time is of the essence.'

'Time is of the essence? Wherever did you pick up a phrase like that?' Bunty shouted down to Butch.

'It was in a film,' he shouted back. 'One cowboy said it to the other as they were galloping across the prairie to rescue a farm from bandits.'

Bunty thought a bit about this before asking, 'Do cowboys gallop then?'

'They do if they're riding a horse,' Butch replied and then, leaning forward in the basket, he howled, 'Ride 'em, cowboy!'

Bunty is right, Eddie thought to himself. His dad had told him to keep out of trouble, and up to now he'd kept his promise. It wasn't his fault that Flo had been kidnapped by a couple of nasties and now he was having to rescue her. Eddie's dad was his best friend, and he hated worrying him, but he'd explain it all on FaceTime when he got home. Feeling less guilty, he pressed on up the steep hill that led to the Knoll.

'I'll teach them to kidnap my friend,' he said angrily, and Bunty, agreeing with him, cried, 'Hear, hear! Onwards and upwards.'

Demonica was shining her torch on the spell book as Dennis held on to Flo and Louis. Slowly she began to chant something in a very strange language.

'Are you sure you're pronouncing that right?' a confused Dennis asked. He'd never heard anything like it. 'Sounds like a load of mumbo jumbo to me.'

'Shurrup,' Demonica hissed. 'You're breaking my concentration.'

Suddenly, the ground began to shake slightly.

'Did you feel that?' a triumphant Demonica screeched. 'It's working!'

Dennis stared at her in disbelief. Even Flo was surprised as something very strange definitely was happening.

For one thing, Demonica's appearance seemed to be changing. She looked bigger and her eyes were the size of saucers, gleaming as black as coal in the light of the full moon as she waved her arms around, gabbling away in this strange language. Finally, she wailed the last part of the chant in something they could understand.

The Pirate Queen has finally arrived,
From across the sea on the evening tide.
So, open your portal, reveal your light,
And let her claim the treasure,
As is her right.

There was a tremendous cracking sound, and for a brief moment the earth shook violently. Slowly the portal began to appear in the side of the Knoll. It looked like a large oval mirror, only instead of glass, the mirror was a pool of shimmering water illuminated by a bright-blue light.

Demonica, shielding her eyes from the light, shouted at Dennis to throw Flo inside. 'Quickly, before it closes again!'

Flo put up a valiant fight, but Dennis had her in a firm grip and there was no way she could get free.

Just as the portal opened wider and the light grew brighter, Eddie arrived at the gate. 'If that's a torch then it's a bright one,' he said in amazement, staring at the light coming from the Knoll. He wheeled his bike into the field and turning full throttle he tore across the grass towards it.

'In you go,' a terrified Dennis stammered as he pushed Flo through the portal. 'Just don't forget the treasure.'

Flo vanished out of sight.

'What the . . .?' Demonica exclaimed as Eddie on his bike, with Stanley following closely behind him, shot past her, following Flo into the portal just as it closed behind them.

There was a deafening silence. Demonica and Dennis just stared at each other, both of them in shock.

'It worked,' Dennis muttered. 'I don't believe it.'

'I told you,' Demonica replied smugly. 'Although, I didn't expect that boy and a crow to show up and go through the portal too. I hope it doesn't interfere with the spell.'

'So, what do we do now?' Dennis asked, shivering slightly as he sat down on the damp grass.

'We wait,' Demonica replied, staring at the moon and smiling happily to herself at the thought of all that lovely treasure, 'until she gets back.'

CHAPTER THIRTY-EIGHT

Just imagine that one minute you're cycling across a field towards a hill, and then a split second later you find yourself skidding to a halt in a tunnel *inside* that hill? I should imagine it would come as a bit of shock, to say the least.

'How did that happen?' a stunned Eddie asked after the portal had closed behind him and he found himself inside a long dark tunnel that had old spidery roots hanging from the roof and smelled of damp earth. 'How did we get inside the Knoll?'

Flo flung her arms round him, much to Eddie's surprise. 'Oh, Eddie,' she cried. 'I'm so glad to see you. You won't believe what's happened!'

'Try me,' Eddie replied, slightly relieved when Flo stopped hugging him.

Flo tried to explain what the Rancid Twins were up to, but even as she spoke, she realised that it all sounded highly improbable. And yet here they were, trapped deep inside a huge mound of earth, after passing through what had looked like a mirror full of water without even getting wet.

Flo suddenly felt bone-tired. It had been a long day, and she was more scared than she cared to admit. Eddie, sensing this, put his arm round her shoulders and gave her a squeeze. This was a gesture that he'd normally shy away from, but it felt like the right thing to do, especially since Flo had given *him* a hug. He felt even closer to her than he had before, as did Flo, who was grateful he was there and didn't feel quite so alone any more.

'Now, let's find a way out of here,' Eddie said. 'There's no reception on my phone, but the torch works and we've got the light from my bike so at least we're not in the dark.'

'Let me fly on ahead,' Stanley suggested. 'This place spooks me out and there might be hidden dangers at the end of this tunnel.'

'I suppose I could burrow through the roof,' Bunty suggested as they slowly made their way down the passage. 'Might take me a bit of time though.'

'I could help. I am a rabbit after all and we're supposed to do that kind of thing,' Louis offered, much to everyone's surprise.

'Although I've never burrowed in my life and I certainly have never lived in a hole in the ground, but I'm happy to help. You are all my comrades, and I shall fight for you until the end.'

'Thank you, Louis,' Eddie replied warmly. 'That's what you call team spirit.'

Butch was growling quietly under his breath as they walked along, his big eyes darting from left to right, in case a bandit should jump out.

It wasn't long before Stanley flew back with news of what was up ahead.

'This tunnel leads to a big circular space; a cavern with lots of other tunnels leading off it,' he told them. 'The problem is, which one are we going to take?'

Surprisingly, and considering the size of the Knoll, it was quite a long walk until they reached the end of the tunnel and came to the cavern.

'Look at this,' Eddie said in a hushed voice as he shone his torch on the domed ceiling. 'It's covered in carvings and funny writing.'

'They're called runes,' Stanley explained. He seemed to have a wealth of knowledge about everything, thought Eddie. 'Magical writing that I'd say, judging by those carvings of longships, were made by the Vikings.'

'Maybe that's who the treasure belonged to,' Eddie said, fascinated. 'Viking invaders.'

'Wrong,' a gruff voice suddenly said, making them all jump.

'I have a feeling we're not alone,' Louis muttered as from out of the tunnels appeared a number of ferocious-looking badgers. They formed a circle round Eddie and Flo, and the biggest badger stepped forward. Eddie stood frozen to the spot as the badger leader started sniffing him.

'Hello,' he said, trying to sound cheerful. 'I'm Eddie Albert. Nice to meet you.'

The badger grunted. 'You understand Badger?'

'Yes I do, as it happens,' Eddie replied, with a bit more confidence. 'And I can understand you.'

The badger laughed. 'Can you now?' he said, scratching his belly. 'A young human Intuitive, eh? And who's this little missy with the rabbit?'

'Tell him your name, Flo,' Eddie said, giving her a little nudge.

'My name is Floortje Anna Maria Antonia Uffen,' she told the badger, hoping that she sounded brave, which isn't easy when you're surrounded by a gang of extremely threatening badgers. 'But everyone calls me Flo.'

'Well, let me introduce myself, my beauties,' the badger said. 'I am the notorious Captain Rascal, executed at Wapping Dock in the year 1700 for Piracy, alongside this gang of rapscallions, otherwise known as my crew.'

'Executed in 1700?' Eddie asked. 'How is that possible?'

'Never mind that,' Captain Rascal said with a sly smile that showed off a frightening amount of teeth. 'Given how you two are dressed, are you supposed to be pirates like us?' He sniggered. 'And is this little Flo the famous Pirate Queen come to claim her treasure?' He fell about laughing, as did all the other badgers.

'What's so funny?' Flo asked angrily. After Eddie explained what the badgers were laughing at, she said, 'You don't look much like pirates yourselves, just a load of badgers who could do with a wash.'

The badgers stopped laughing then, and Captain Rascal stepped closer to Flo.

'Is that so,' he said menacingly, making Flo wince from

the smell of his breath. 'Let me explain something to you,' he began. 'You might have heard the legend of how the treasure is guarded by the ghosts of thirteen drowned pirates? Well, you see, little missy, that's us. We're the drowned pirates, doomed to inhabit the bodies of badgers until the end of time, guarding the treasure and the entrance to the Realm of Faerie against intruders like you.'

Eddie translated, and all Flo could say was, 'Oh.' Things were getting stranger down here by the second. Did Eddie really just tell her that these badgers guarded fairy-land?

'Spell faerie,' Captain Rascal suddenly asked Flo.

Eddie repeated his request and nervously she spelled out FAIRY.

'Wrong,' the badger replied. 'You spell it F A E R I E, that's the old and proper way of spelling it. Remember that, missy.'

'So then, what are we going to do with this lot, Cap'n?' a badger who went by the name of Fish-Guts, asked. 'Rip them to pieces?'

The rest of the badgers murmured their approval.

'Yes,' a fearsome-looking badger called Barnacle Pete snarled. 'Tear 'em apart and leave what's left of 'em for the foxes and the crows.'

'What a disgusting thing to suggest,' Stanley said. 'As if you'd catch me doing anything like that.'

'Oh dear,' Bunty moaned, as the badgers moved closer towards them. 'If only Dan and Jake were here, they might be able to reason with this lot.'

'Dan and Jake?' a surprised Captain Rascal asked, stopping in his tracks. 'Do you mean Dan and Jake the goldfish?'

'Yes, they live with me,' Eddie replied, more than a little surprised himself. 'Why? Have you heard of them?'

This set all the badgers off into fits of laughter.

'Have we heard of them?' Captain Rascal roared once he'd managed to stop laughing. 'Did you hear that, lads? Why they're only two of the most fearsome and infamous pirates to ever sail the seven seas.'

Eddie was dumbfounded. 'Really?' he asked, unable to believe his ears. 'Dan and Jake? My two goldfish?'

'That's right, my lad, and any friend of Dan and Jake's is a friend of ours,' Captain Rascal said cheerfully. 'Now, how can we help you?'

'What's made them turn so friendly all of a sudden?' Flo asked.

'They know Dan and Jake,' Eddie replied.

'*The fish?!*' Flo was even more surprised than Eddie.

'That's right, the fish, but don't ask me to explain, just be thankful that they've changed their minds about tearing us to pieces,' he said, breathing a sigh of relief as he began to explain to Captain Rascal how they came to be inside the Knoll, and all about the villainous twins.

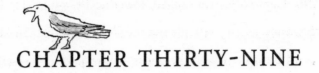

CHAPTER THIRTY-NINE

'As rotten as a bucket of ten-day-old fish-heads,' Captain Rascal declared after listening to Eddie's story. 'We'll have to do something about that pair, they need to be taught a lesson.'

'So, how do we get out of here?' Eddie asked, aware that Aunt Budge was probably going frantic with worry. 'We really need to get home.'

'Ah, well, you see I'm afraid that won't be possible. Once you're inside the Knoll, you can never leave.'

This news caused a lot of fuss and they all began to panic.

'But there must be some way out?' Eddie implored the badger. 'Surely there's a tunnel or something that we can use?'

'I'm afraid not. The only way out is with Kalen's permission, and he has only ever given that once, as far as I know, and that was years ago.'

'Who's Kalen? Another badger?'

'No,' Captain Rascal replied, lowering his voice. 'He is a faerie prince, a fierce warrior and the favourite of Queen Mab. He must be treated with the greatest of respect as he can be extremely dangerous. Would you like me to summon him?'

Eddie nodded in agreement as any chance to get out of here was better than no chance at all.

'Blow the horn, Fish-Guts.' Captain Rascal gave the order.

'Is that wise, boss?' an extremely wary Fish-Guts asked. 'We haven't called upon him in ages.'

'Well, now is the time,' Captain Rascal said firmly. 'Blow the horn, Fish-Guts, Captain's orders.'

'Aye aye, Cap'n,' Fish-Guts replied, and taking a ram's horn down from the wall, he blew hard.

'I can't hear anything,' Flo whispered to Eddie. 'Maybe it's broken.'

Badgers have very good hearing, and Captain Rascal, overhearing what Flo had said, told Eddie that only those who dwelt in the faerie realm could hear it.

They waited in silence for something to happen, and then, after what seemed like an age, two very large dogs emerged from the darkness, setting Butch off barking. The dogs ignored Butch and stood silently on either side of the entrance to one of the larger tunnels.

Eddie could feel his heart pounding in his chest as he waited for something more to happen, and without any warning it did, as a man suddenly appeared, as if out of nowhere. It was Kalen, the warrior prince himself. He was tall and handsome with piercing green eyes and long, wavy red hair, and he was dressed in a suit of silver armour. The only clue that he was a

faerie was the pair of translucent wings on his back that shone like a rainbow in the light of Eddie's bike.

The badgers bowed low and Eddie, Flo and the animals, following their example, did the same.

'Thank you, my lord, for answering our call,' Captain Rascal said reverently. 'We are indeed honoured by your presence.'

'I was wondering if you'd summon me,' Kalen said, patting one of the big dogs' heads. 'There has been much talk in the kingdom of a portal opening. Are these human children and their animals responsible for this?' he demanded, frowning at Eddie and Flo.

'In a way . . . Your Highness.' Eddie stumbled over his words as he tried to explain to this magical presence what had happened. 'You see, we didn't want to be here. Flo was forced in here and then I sort of followed, and erm, well . . .'

'Let me explain to the prince,' Captain Rascal quickly intervened. He told Kalen everything that Eddie had told him.

Kalen studied them for a while before speaking. 'We have ancient rules here that must never be broken, and those who enter a sacred faerie hill can never leave.'

'But it's not our fault,' Flo protested. 'We don't even want to be here.'

'However,' Kalen continued, raising his voice slightly, 'yours are unusual circumstances, and so your case must be put before the Faerie Council. They will decide your fate. Now, follow me.'

CHAPTER FORTY

hat struck both Eddie and Flo was that despite the fantastical situation they'd landed in, it all seemed, somehow, well, strangely normal. They were standing in what appeared to be an enormous library with shelves of books reaching up so high it was impossible to see where they ended, if they ever did.

'The Great Hall of Records,' Captain Rascal whispered to Eddie as they entered this amazing place. 'Everything that's ever taken place in the faerie world is recorded here.'

'Then a lot must've happened to fill that lot,' Eddie replied, awed at the number of books there were.

'They go all the way back to the dawn of time,' Captain Rascal told him. 'And beautifully illustrated as well, or so I'm told,' he added, never having read one.

Kalen was talking to a group of faeries who were sitting behind a bench. This bench was so high that Kalen had to fly up to talk to them, his wings flapping so fast that they were virtually invisible. Flo and Eddie were blown away at the sight of an actual faerie flying right in front of their very eyes, and Stanley was impressed as well. He let out a whistle exclaiming, 'Now they're what you call some pretty cool, high-powered wings.'

There were six faeries assembled behind the bench, and Kalen was deep in conversation with the faerie who was sat in the middle of them. She seemed to be very important, dressed entirely in gold and wearing a garland of flowers on top of her head. When she spoke, she reminded Eddie of a high court judge that he'd seen on TV.

'You must agree, My Lady Astraea,' Eddie could hear Kalen saying. 'These mortal children are the innocent parties here. The real culprits are the ones who opened the portal in the first place and forced them in here to retrieve the treasure.'

Lady Astraea laughed. 'Then it's lucky that our treasure is locked away safely,' she said smiling, 'otherwise, this pair of dangerous buccaneers might have run off with it.'

'Oh, but we're not interested in your treasure,' Flo said in an anxious voice.

'And we're not buccaneers, either. We were at the Ollington

Village Fête, and this is fancy dress,' Eddie added. 'We just want to go home.'

'I know all about the fête; the faeries were observing you,'

Lady Astraea told them kindly. 'And I realise that you are here against your wish, but the ancient rule that commands you to stay cannot be broken. Unless, of course—'

'Rules are rules,' one of the other faeries interrupted.

'That's Lord Rigourex,' Captain Rascal whispered. 'He is older than the others by two hundred years.'

He also looks extremely angry, Eddie thought.

'It clearly states in book three hundred and fifty-six of the Faerie Code that intruders can never be allowed to leave, nor can they stay here. Instead, they must be banished to the Underland,' Rigourex added firmly.

This statement caused quite a fuss and it set the faeries arguing among themselves.

'If you recall, My Lord, a young mortal who had helped a faerie in distress was allowed to leave and return to the mortal world,' another faerie reminded him.

'But that was many years ago, Grundy,' Lord Rigourex replied in a huff. 'And the circumstances were entirely different. No, I say these young mortals be banished to the Underland.'

'I think that's a bit much,' a faerie who was busy knitting said, shaking her head in disagreement. 'The Underland is a dreadful place that only an old misery would banish two young mortals and their animals to.'

'Are you calling me an old misery, Faerie Freya?' Lord Rigourex looked as if he were about to explode. 'Do you have a better suggestion?'

'I'd turn them into a beautiful pair of doves and set them free,' Faerie Freya said dreamily before tutting to herself as she realised she'd dropped a stitch.

'Why doves?' one of the younger faeries offered. 'Why not just let them go as they are. They're no danger to us.'

'Rules are rules,' Lord Rigourex shouted again. 'And you, Faerie Wilda, are far too young to have an opinion about such a serious matter.'

'Well, I think we should bend the rules,' Faerie Wilda argued. 'Let them go home, but cast a memory spell on them first.'

'Well, I don't approve of your modern ideas,' Lord Rigourex snapped back. 'Memory spells indeed. Where did you learn that, Faerie Wilda? At school?'

'At least I'm not still living in the seventh century,' she retorted. 'Unlike some people I could mention who should've retired from the bench years ago and taken up residence in a toadstool home in the woods.'

'How dare you address an Elder like that? Carry on that way, young faerie, and you'll be taking a trip to the Underland yourself.'

'Order,' Lady Astraea shouted, standing up and banging her wooden staff – cut from a hawthorn tree and said to possess magical powers – on the floor. 'I have listened to you all and have come to a decision that is only fair and right. The mortal children shall return to the mortal world.'

Faerie Wilda cheered, but Lord Rigourex was less impressed. 'I object,' he protested.

'Objection overruled,' Lady Astraea told him firmly. 'I've made my decision and my decision is final. They shall go free. But I do think we should teach the two mortals who opened the portal a lesson – stop them from ever doing it again. I think you'd agree with that, Lord Rigourex?' she asked the angry faerie, who nodded grumpily.

'Take these to the children,' she said to Kalen, handing him two leather pouches. 'And on their return to the human world, they are to give them to the Rancid Twins and instruct them to enter the portal if they want to claim the treasure.'

Kalen couldn't understand her reasoning. Why would she allow two wicked humans to enter the Knoll? She must have something up her sleeve, he thought, as he flew down to Flo and Eddie to give them their instructions.

'Thank you,' a relieved Eddie and Flo both told Lady Astraea.

'And we won't tell anyone what we've seen here. We promise, don't we, Flo?' Eddie assured the faerie.

'I know you won't,' Lady Astraea replied. 'Because after a minute or so of leaving here, you won't remember a thing. You'll forget all that you've witnessed.'

'Nice knowing you,' Captain Rascal said, holding out a paw for Eddie to shake. 'Don't forget to say hello to Dan and Jake from me. Oh, wait,' he added. 'You won't be able to as you'll have forgotten. Never mind!'

Lady Astraea held out her staff and waved it in the air. The same oval shape appeared, identical to the one that they'd entered through.

'Go in peace,' Lady Astraea said as they walked towards the portal. 'And Eddie, you possess a magical talent. Use it wisely and one day in the future, you will be able to benefit both the Kingdom of the Animals and mankind.'

'Thanks for not stepping on the bluebells, Flo,' Faerie Wilda said, giving Flo a big wink. 'Good luck will always follow you for that.'

And within a split second, they were back outside the Knoll.

'Well?' Demonica squealed as she rushed at them. 'Where's the treasure? Where is it?'

Eddie and Flo handed over the two leather pouches that Lady Astraea had given them. Demonica snatched both of them, and there was quite a squabble between her and Dennis until he grabbed back one of them for himself.

'What is it?' Demonica drooled as she reached into the pouch. Pulling out the biggest, shiniest ruby that she'd ever seen, she let out a loud squeal of delight. 'Oh, be still my wicked heart,' she gasped, for the ruby was the size of a tennis ball.

Dennis could barely speak. His bag contained a vivid green emerald that glowed in the moonlight. 'Rio, here I come,' he sighed, glassy-eyed.

'Lady Astraea told us to give these to you,' Eddie explained. 'She's a faerie, and she said if you want more, then you'll have to go inside the Knoll and get it yourselves.'

The portal they'd returned through had vanished, but as Eddie spoke another one appeared. This one was different though, as there was no blue light. Instead, this portal was darker and the light from inside shone a deep red.

'Get out of my way,' Demonica screamed, pushing Dennis aside, 'and let me get my hands on that treasure.'

'Half of it is mine,' Dennis reminded her, grabbing her by the arm and pulling her back so he could get to the portal before her.

'That's what you think,' she retorted, jumping on to his back and covering his eyes with her hand.

'Gerroff me,' he cried, staggering around as he tried to shake her off.

Lil the sheep had been watching all this, and seeing her chance, she charged and butted both of them hard, sending the pair of them hurtling through the portal.

'I feel better for that,' a satisfied Lil said, as the portal closed behind them. 'Good riddance to bad rubbish.'

'Let's get out of here in case they come back,' Eddie said to Flo, but as he spoke he found that his legs felt heavy and he was suddenly very tired.

'Just let me sit down for a minute,' Flo said, yawning loudly. 'I need to rest for a . . .' but she never got to finish what she was saying as she'd fallen into a deep sleep.

Bunty, Louis, Stanley and Butch were already fast asleep.

Butch was snoring his head off, curled up next to Louis and Bunty. Eddie, unable to keep his eyes open any longer, found himself lying down on the grass too, and quickly drifted off to sleep.

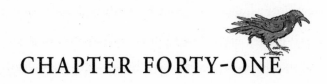

CHAPTER FORTY-ONE

'Wake up,' a familiar voice was saying. 'Where have you been? I've been worried sick. Wake up!'

Eddie smiled. This was a strange dream to be having in the middle of such a lovely sleep.

'Wake up!' the voice ordered again, and realising that it wasn't a dream and that someone was shaking him, Eddie slowly opened his eyes.

'Where am I?' he asked as he tried to focus, blinking hard in the bright light of a torch that the someone was holding. 'Who are you?' he asked the shadow.

'It's me, Aunt Budge,' she replied angrily. 'And what are you doing here on the Knoll fast asleep, may I ask? You haven't been drinking or talking illegal substances, I hope. Oh dear me, what would your father say? He'd say I was a stupid old woman and never allow me to see you again,' she wailed.

When Eddie hadn't returned home, and as there'd been no

news from the police about Flo's whereabouts, Aunt Budge had told Whetstone to get the car out, and together with Miss Schmidt they'd set out to search for them. Giddy and Jacob had arrived on their way back from France, and Aunt Budge had asked them to stay in the cottage in case Eddie and Flo returned.

Luckily, as they drove around the lanes, they'd spotted the black van that belonged to the Rancid Twins parked by the gate of the field that led to the Knoll. And this was how they'd found Eddie, Flo and the animals – all of them fast asleep.

'Please tell me you haven't done anything silly?' Aunt Budge implored them both.

'We haven't been doing anything silly, have we, Flo?' Eddie said, turning to Flo who was now sitting up with a dazed expression on her face. 'We're not stupid.'

'Then what are you doing here and in this state?' Aunt Budge asked, more concerned than angry now.

Eddie tried to think, but to his surprise he couldn't remember what he was doing on the Knoll, no matter how hard he tried, and neither could Flo or the animals.

'I can't remember a thing,' Flo admitted with a worried look. 'I can remember being at the fête and then . . .' she paused as she tried hard to remember something. 'And then, nothing at all.'

'Same here,' Eddie agreed. 'I can't think of a thing.'

'Amnesia,' Miss Schmidt suddenly announced with authority. 'We need to get them home and into the warm. The air smells of snow.'

'Oh, don't be ridiculous, Miss Schmidt,' Aunt Budge said as she helped Flo up. 'Snow? At this time of year?'

Whetstone was waiting with the car by the gate. He'd rung the police to tell them that Eddie and Flo had been found safe, and that there was no need to worry.

'But what about those awful kidnappers, Flo?' Aunt Budge asked as they drove home. 'What happened to them?'

'What kidnappers?' a puzzled Flo asked. 'I don't remember that.'

'But the alpacas told Eddie that you and Louis had been kidnapped!' Aunt Budge said, equally puzzled. 'Surely you remember that?'

'No,' was all Flo could say, and Louis nodded in agreement.

'How strange,' Aunt Budge sighed. 'I don't know what to think, I really don't.'

'I've told you before,' Miss Schmidt reminded her. 'Amnesia.'

'I don't know what this amnesia thing is,' Bunty muttered to

Eddie. 'But if one of the symptoms is hunger, then I've got it. I'm famished, and I want my dinner.'

'We'll soon be home,' Eddie reassured her, and they drove down the hill, leaving the Knoll and all of its mysteries behind them.

As soon as they all got home, Aunt Budge insisted that a doctor was called, and after examining both Flo and Eddie, he declared that there was absolutely nothing wrong with either of them, almost accusing Aunt Budge of wasting his time.

'Doctors,' Miss Schmidt remarked grumpily after she'd seen him out. 'What do they know? I still say it's amnesia.'

Aunt Budge, only now realising that Flo and Eddie still had their costumes on, told them to go and get changed.

'I can't wait to get these boots off,' Eddie said, as he and Flo headed upstairs. 'There must be a stone or something inside, it's killing me.'

'Me too!' Flo agreed. 'I think I've got a stone in my shoe as well.'

But it wasn't a stone at all, and when Eddie and Flo removed their footwear, they discovered that the source of their discomfort was, in fact, a couple of gold doubloons.

'Wow,' Eddie cried in amazement. 'Pirate gold. Where did these come from?'

'I've no idea,' Flo replied, turning the heavy gold coin over in the palm of her hand. 'But they must be worth a fortune.' And they both shot downstairs to show Aunt Budge.

'She's outside with Giddy,' Jacob told them. He was sitting quietly by himself in the big armchair. 'They're looking at the moon; it's full tonight.'

'Look what we've got,' Eddie said, holding his hand out for Jacob to take a look at the doubloon. 'We've both got one.'

Jacob smiled as he examined the coins. 'You know what I think?' he said with a twinkle in his eye. 'I'd say that this was pirate gold that once belonged to the faeries, but don't quote me on that,' he added with a wink.

'You'll never guess what?' Giddy exclaimed as she burst into the room. 'It's snowing outside.'

Could this night get any stranger? Eddie thought to himself as he rushed outside with Flo and Butch to take a look.

And so it was, it was snowing and quite heavily.

'Can you believe this peculiar weather?' Aunt Budge said, holding her hand out to catch the snowflakes. 'And at this time of year as well.'

'Isn't it lovely?' Giddy said. 'And tomorrow's Easter Sunday, so happy Easter everyone!' she shouted, and they all cheered. Even Louis was enjoying himself, chasing Butch around, kicking up his hind legs and covering him in soft powdery snow.

Jacob, watching their antics from the window, chuckled to himself as he took a gold doubloon out of his waistcoat pocket that was exactly the same as Eddie and Flo's.

'Faerie gold,' he said, smiling that secret smile again as he rubbed the coin between his fingers, the coin that he'd been given as a reward by Kalen many years ago when he was just a teenager, for helping a faerie that had been cornered by a dog.

The faeries had cast a memory spell on Jacob, just as they had on Eddie and Flo, and for years he couldn't remember a thing about his experiences. However, as he grew older, he began to have strange dreams and flashbacks, until the morning of his ninety-eighth birthday, when he woke up to find that he could remember the whole thing as if it were yesterday.

This made him think that the older you got, the more the spell faded, eventually losing its power and restoring the memory completely. He'd mentioned his encounter with the faeries to Giddy, but it was obvious that she didn't believe him, thinking that it was just the ramblings of a very old man whose mind and memory weren't quite what they used to be.

But there was nothing wrong with either Jacob's mind or his memory, and as he watched Eddie and Flo throwing snowballs at each other, he hoped that when they grew old, they too would start to remember the faeries of Ollington Knoll.

'Gotcha,' Aunt Budge shouted, hurtling a snowball at Whetstone and knocking his cap off.

'Would madam permit me to retaliate and throw a snowball back at her?' he asked, picking his cap up and dusting the snow off the peak.

'Of course, you silly man,' Aunt Budge said, getting ready to throw another one. 'That's what snowball fights are all about. You can't play it on your own. Now *en garde*!' she shouted, and before long they were pelting each other with snowballs.

'You know something, Eddie Albert?' Flo sighed as she watched Whetstone and Aunt Budge chasing each other around the garden like a couple of five-year-olds. 'Amsterdam's going to feel very boring after this.'

'Course it won't,' Eddie replied. 'But I'm going to miss you. As well as Aunt Budge and everyone else of course,' he added quickly.

'That's good,' Flo said. 'You're my best friend.'

'Am I?' Eddie couldn't have been more surprised, as nobody had ever called him their best friend before. He felt a sudden rush of happiness and blurted out, 'Well, you're my best friend as well.'

'That's good then,' Flo replied, laughing at the expression on his face. 'Now, let's have a snowball fight,' she said, and they ran off to join the others.

Miss Schmidt, watching the snow falling from her kitchen window as she happily battered a lump of dough, had only this to say:

'I knew it would snow.' And, highly satisfied that her prediction had come true, she added. 'I'm never wrong.'

And she very rarely was.

FIRST EPILOGUE

Of course, you've probably guessed that the portal the Rancid Twins went through wasn't the same one that Eddie and Flo had gone through. Unfortunately for the twins, this portal led to the place known as the Underland, and not to the smugglers' treasure. Once the portal had closed behind them, they discovered to their horror that the ruby and the emerald in the leather pouches had transformed into nothing more than two lumps of coal.

'I think we've been tricked,' Dennis moaned as he gazed mournfully at the coal. 'But I don't know how the trick was done.'

'Never mind that,' Demonica snarled. 'How do we get out of here?'

'I'm afraid you don't,' a voice in the darkness replied. 'You're here for eternity.' And stepping out of the shadows, Kalen appeared. 'Let me escort you to the Underland, your trial is about to begin,' he said grimly. 'Follow me.'

However, five years later, the faeries, having grown tired of the twins' constant arguing and fighting, had thrown them out, and the pair were found wandering around the village in the early hours of the morning, dazed and confused with no idea where they had been. The police were called, and after a night in the cells they were put on a train out of the county and were never seen again.

Old Molly Maggot's house was demolished, having been quite rightly condemned as a danger to public safety, and today there's no trace of it left.

SECOND EPILOGUE

'Well, I was dubious at first when you said let's paint the kitchen orange, but I have to say that it's growing on me. In fact, I quite like it,' Eddie's dad said as they sat at the table in the newly painted kitchen.

'I told you that orange was the right colour,' Eddie replied proudly as he munched on the Easter egg that his dad had given him when he got home. 'And it looks super cool with the new kitchen cupboards you've painted bright blue.'

Eddie was glad to be home. He'd had a wonderful time with Aunt Budge, even if there were parts of the holiday that he just couldn't remember, no matter how hard he tried.

'So, tell me,' his dad asked, helping himself to a piece of the Easter egg. 'What did you get up to down there in Kent? Aunt Budge said you were no trouble at all and had a marvellous time. What's the old girl doing next?'

'She's staying in Kent for the time being,' Eddie said, licking chocolate off his fingers. 'And then she said something about going to India. I hope she asks me and Flo to go with her.'

Eddie's dad raised his eyebrows when he heard this. Amsterdam and Kent were one thing, but India? He'd have to think about that one.

'So, come on then,' he urged, changing the subject from India back to the Romney Marshes. 'Tell me all about the exciting things you did.'

'Well, me and Flo went out a lot on our bikes and visited a place called Dungeness on a miniature railway, and what else? Oh yes, we went to the fairground and we . . .' Eddie struggled to remember what else had happened. '. . . And I nearly forgot, I played the electric guitar at the village fête.'

'What?! You mean you actually got up on stage and played in front of people?' His dad was more than a bit shocked, as Eddie had never had the confidence to do this before. 'How did that happen? Tell me more.' He pressed Eddie eagerly, grinning from ear to ear.

'We all dressed up as pirates and Aunt Budge got up and sang. The band weren't able to make it, but as they'd got their instruments set up, Aunt Budge made us all play with her,' Eddie said. 'Flo played the trumpet.'

'Eddie Albert,' his dad exclaimed proudly. 'You never cease to amaze me. What happened to my shy little boy who wouldn't say boo to a goose? What else did you get up to?'

'I met Aunt Budge's friends, who were very nice, and then me and Flo went exploring around the Knoll . . .' As soon as he mentioned the Knoll, a strange feeling came over him, as if something had happened, but he couldn't remember what it was. All he remembered was Aunt Budge waking them up from a deep sleep and the mystery of the gold coins that both he and Flo had found in their boots. Where had they come from? It really was a mystery, and a strange one, which is why he wasn't going to mention the coin to his dad, as he just couldn't explain it.

'What's the Knoll?' his dad asked.

'Oh, just an old hill,' Eddie replied casually, picking Bunty up from the kitchen table before she could get her teeth into the Easter egg. 'D'you mind if I go up to my room?'

'Not at all,' his dad replied. 'Oh, and, Eddie,' he added with a wink as Eddie got up to leave, 'it's good to have you home. I've missed you.'

Eddie smiled, but he didn't blush this time as he usually did when his dad said something soppy. Instead, he returned his dad's wink and said, 'I missed you as well, Dad. It's nice to be home.' And vanishing behind the kitchen door he ran up the stairs to his room to put the coin away somewhere safe.

Stanley, perched on the kitchen windowsill outside, remembered everything that had happened on the Knoll as, unlike Eddie, Flo, Louis, Bunty and Butch, the memory spell that the faeries had cast on them didn't work on birds. Even so, worried that revealing any information would anger the faeries of the Knoll, who might then take revenge, he'd decided to keep his beak well and truly shut and put the entire episode behind him.

'Best let sleeping dogs lie,' he croaked as he took off across the park to see if there was anything going on. 'Say nothing, I say.'

And do you know what? He never did.